FORBIDDEN WORLD

Captain Smooth swallowed two or three times and squinted at Ben Brasken.

"Where have you been?" he asked.

"Ost," Ben Brasken said. "I just told you."

"How did you get there?"

"I swam."

"How did you get back?"

"I swam."

"What did you find there, Ben Brasken?"

Ben Braskin shut his eyes and seemed to be thinking.

"I believe," he said grimly, "the main thing I found was the awful terror."

Bantam Books by Kenneth Robeson
Ask your bookseller for the books you have missed

About Doc Savage®

DOC SAVAGE: HIS APOCALYPTIC LIFE
by Philip José Farmer

THE MAGIC ISLAND

(Formerly published as OST)

A DOC SAVAGE® ADVENTURE

BY KENNETH ROBESON

THE MAGIC ISLAND

*A Bantam Book / published by arrangement with
The Condé Nast Publications Inc.*

Formerly published as OST

PRINTING HISTORY
*Originally published August 1937
in DOC SAVAGE Magazine
Bantam edition / July 1977*

ISBN 0–553–07790–2

Published simultaneously in the United States and Canada

CONTENTS

Chapter I

THE CITY THAT WAS NOT THERE

It was remarkable that anything Ben Brasken did should astound the world.

Ben Brasken was what is sometimes called "a poor fish." This had no connection with his being a sailor. He was meek, abused, and did not have many manly qualities of the hairy-chested kind. He was short. He was thin. He had never won a fight, although he had had several. He was as poor as a church mouse, and somewhat resembled one. Not that he went to church. They did not have a church on the *Benny Boston*. All they had was grease, heat, smell, hard work and a hard skipper and a first mate with bucko leanings.

Ben Brasken had one quality. It was this one thing that got him into all his trouble. And got some other people into theirs. Which also caused some heads to turn gray, and a few people to die.

To say nothing of the incredible chain of things it started happening.

A dreamer, this Ben Brasken. Not a student. Not a wise man. He read a lot, though. Most of his reading was simple stuff about heroes who were everything Ben Brasken was not. None of it was deep. What he read went in one eye and out the other. At any rate, he was kind of a dumb cluck.

Most of the time, he dreamed. He would stop and lean on his shovel and go off in reveries until somebody threw a chunk of coal at him. Ben Brasken was a fireman on the *Benny Boston*. The *Benny Boston* was a small tramp freighter, nearly as old as Ben Brasken, who was not a young man any more. It was a wonder the *Benny Boston* got by the inspectors.

Ben Brasken's dreams worried nobody but his employers, and didn't worry them much, because Ben Brasken wasn't worth worrying about. He was paid his not-very-good keep—a hammock in the creaking fo'c's'le, and a few of Uncle Sam's dollars each month, a very few.

Not that Ben Brasken was what is variously called a

1

goop, a nut, bats in his belfry, or strange. Not a bit of it. Ben Brasken was just a poor failure of a sailor man who got his joy out of life by standing around, or going off in some corner where he was alone, and dreaming. They were light, harmless little dreams about Rolls Royces, penthouses, mints of money, and pretty girls. Just things he had seen in the movies.

An understanding of Ben Brasken, the kind of sailor man he was, is necessary to understand the fantastic things he started happening.

Soon after Ben Brasken shipped for his first voyage on the sea-going coffin, *Benny Boston,* he knew something was wrong.

The other sailors. They stood around in knots. When Ben Brasken, who was a sociable mouse in a quiet way, came up to them, they would stop talking and split up. They had a secret among them, and didn't want to share it.

Rough seas, a stinking tub of a ship, and hard work are wonderful ice-breakers where conversation is concerned, though. On the eleventh day out of San Francisco, destination New Guinea and other South Seas islands, a sailor told Ben Brasken what was what. The sailor had just polished off a pint he had smuggled aboard in San Francisco, but that was of no importance.

In truth, Ben Brasken did not give the story the credence he should have. He thought it was a little goofy.

"Say, what's the big secret around here?" Ben Brasken asked.

You see, his conversation was perfectly rational.

"Ah, it's somethin' most of us figure we saw on the last voyage," explained the sailor. "The skipper got mad and said he'd beach any sailor he caught talkin' about it. The skipper thinks he's got dignity. He don't want to get to be known as one of these captains who sight sea monsters.

"Everybody knows there ain't no sea monsters. Anybody who says he seen one is either a liar or tryin' to get his name in the papers, the skipper claims. See how it is? The old man don't want people to start laughin' at his boat."

Ben Brasken was naturally interested. "What did you see?"

The sailor squinted one eye and sucked his upper teeth. "I ain't sayin' we saw anythin'. It's what we thought we saw. It was a city."

"A city?"

"Yeah. It was at sea, at night. It was as dark as hell, and everybody knows you can't see anythin' when it is dark. But these buildin's in this city was there plain as could be. They showed up kinda like the stuff on the kind of watches you can tell time by in the dark."

"A mirage," said Ben Brasken.

"Huh?"

"A mirage. You see 'em in the deserts, and sometimes at sea."

"It was dark."

"Oh! Then it must have been phosphorescence in the water. You see a lot of that in the South Seas."

"This city was kinda up in the sky."

Ben Brasken scratched his head. He was baffled. "Where was this?"

"Two hundred miles off the New Guinea coast."

"That was kinda queer, wasn't it?" Ben Brasken said, after a minute. "How do you explain it?"

"Well, the skipper said it must be somebody on another boat throwin' a magic-lantern picture on a cloud. He said they use powerful magic lanterns and throw advertising pictures and stuff on clouds in New York and places like that."

"Of course!" exclaimed Ben Brasken. "That explains it."

The other snorted. "It don't explain how we all knew the name of the city was Ost."

"You what?"

"Everybody who saw the city knew it was called Ost. Don't ask me how. We can't figure it out. Yet somehow, every man knew it was Ost."

"That's funny."

"It get still funnier when you know there ain't no city named Ost."

"There ain't?"

"No, there ain't. We looked on all the charts."

Ben Brasken was not without a sense of humor. He did not believe in such spooky tales. He was sure fortune tellers were fakes, mediums were hoodoos, and anybody who believed in spiritualism was only kidding himself. So Ben Brasken burst out laughing.

"How'd you like a bust in the snoot?" growled the other, offended.

That put an end to it.

Until, of course, Ben Brasken disappeared at sea.

WHEN Ben Brasken was missed, and the cry, "Man overboard!" rang through the ancient *Benny Boston,* it was too late for there to be any hope.

Anyway, every one aboard was in something of a dither, because the glowing city in the sky had been seen again. The watch below, loitering on the murky foredeck, discovered it first.

A sailor ran to get the skipper, whose name was Captain Smooth, a name, incidentally, which did not fit him.

The sailor met Ben Brasken in a companionway, and shouted, "We're seein' that thing again!"

"I know it," Ben Brasken replied. "I am on my way there now."

That was the last they saw of Ben Brasken on that voyage. A rain squall hit the old steamer a few minutes later, and while a rain squall is nothing to a good ocean freighter, when one blew down on the *Benny Boston,* things had to be watched. All hands were busy for a while, and they stopped seeing the city.

They they missed Ben Brasken. They searched the fo'c's'le, the other places where he might logically be, and didn't find him.

The sailor who had met Ben Brasken on the companion got to thinking.

"He said he was on his way there," the seaman muttered. "Holy ladders! I wonder if he meant he was on his way to that city? I thought he meant he was headed for the deck to have a look."

Captain Smooth ordered the *Benny Boston* hove to.

They laid there the rest of the night, the vessel rolling, and some of the men became seasick. Yes, sailors get seasick.

The day dawned bright and clear. There was no city in sight. There was just a lot of ocean.

They did not find poor Ben Brasken.

They sailed on to Melbourne, Australia, which was as far as they went. In Melbourne, the story got out, and the newspapers ate it up. Captain Smooth got a cable from his owners telling him to cut out such idiocy.

When they returned to San Francisco, some enterprising reporters got the first mate tight, and the front pages carried his remarks.

Captain Smooth was carpeted, the *Benny Boston* got a new first mate, and became an old-fashioned hellship on the leg back to Melbourne. It helped a little when they didn't see the strange city.

But they saw the city when three hundred miles off the New Guinea coast, enroute back to San Francisco.

And they found Ben Brasken climbing aboard the *Benny Boston* in the open sea, carrying an iron block.

BEN BRASKEN hauled himself over the rail, and stood, clothes leaking water, holding his piece of iron. The rope up which he had climbed was a line which trailed overside and down into the water.

The first two sailors to see Ben Brasken lit out running, reached the fo'c's'le, and didn't say a word. They thought they had seen a ghost.

And why not? Ben Brasken had vanished quite some time ago in the open sea, and here he was climbing aboard again! On the face of the thing, it was absolutely impossible.

Captain Smooth, when Ben Brasken was brought before him, took three fingers of rum in a water glass, although he was not a drinking man. Before he said a word, Captain Smooth looked for a long time at the sailor who had done the impossible.

A different Ben Brasken stood before him, yet it was the same man, or a shadow of the same man.

Ben Brasken was emaciated, so thin that the shape of

his teeth actually showed under his cheeks and lips when his mouth was closed. His eyes were burning coals.

Water ran off him and made a pool on the old rug in the captain's cabin.

Captain Smooth looked at Ben Brasken's piece of iron.

The piece of iron was less than a foot long, less than half that wide, a little less thick than it was wide, and had a kind of handle fastened to one flat side. The other flat side was smooth.

In general, it was rather like an oversize flatiron of the old-fashioned kind that had to be heated on the cookstove. Except that it had squarish ends.

When Captain Smooth got a voice, he pointed at the iron and asked, "What's that?"

"An ordinary piece of iron," Ben Brasken replied hollowly. "But it was touched with the magic of the mighty Goa, and so with this key I was able to walk through the mouth of the cave into Ost."

Captain Smooth swallowed two or three times and squinted at Ben Brasken.

"Where have you been?" he asked.

"Ost," Ben Brasken said. "I just told you."

"How did you get there?"

"I swam."

"How did you get back?"

"I swam."

"What did you find there, Ben Brasken?"

Ben Brasken shut his eyes and seemed to be thinking.

"I believe," he said grimly, "the main thing I found was the awful terror."

CAPTAIN SMOOTH sat back, relaxed, and tried to look as gentle as he could. He was suddenly convinced that he was dealing with a demented man.

"What is Ost?" Captain Smooth asked quietly. "We'd like to know all about your experiences, Ben. Is Ost a town on one of the Japanese islands?"

"No," Ben Brasken replied quickly, "Ost is the city

of the Ostians. The Japs probably never heard of it. You never heard of it either, did you?"

"I—I think I saw it in the sky," Captain Smooth said. "It was kind of a glowing color."

"The buildings were shaped like pyramids?" Ben Brasken asked. "And one of them, the temple of Goa the mighty, was upside down?"

Captain Smooth gulped. As a matter of fact, one of the queer aspects of the city in the sky had been the apparent upside-down position of one huge building.

The city, as he and the crew had observed it, had been somewhat vague as to outline, and the exact details of the structures did not stand out any too clearly.

"What was this horror you mentioned?" Captain Smooth asked.

Ben Brasken seemed to think again.

"It was so terrible," he said at last, "that you had better give me time to think of a way to describe it so you will understand."

"That's all right, Ben," Captain Smooth said quickly. "Take your time. What else did you see?"

"I saw Martin Space."

"Oh, then the people in Ost are white people, eh?"

"No. Martin Space is a white man. And there was a woman, who was also white. The rest were Ostians."

"What do the Ostians look like?"

Ben Brasken had to think over that, too. "I guess, when I first saw them, I thought of them as the spider-armed men."

"Eh?"

"The spider-armed men. They have blue bodies, too."

The skipper suddenly decided he had enough of this. Ben Brasken looked so inhuman that talking to him was not a pleasure.

"Well, well, Ben, this is all very interesting, and I know I want to hear more about it," he said. "But you must be tired, and now I want you to have a good long rest. You can have a cabin all to yourself, and we will just lock the door so no one will be bothering you."

Ben Brasken became animated.

"No, no!" he cried out vehemently. "You must turn

and go to Ost at once! That is why I am here. I came to get you to save Ost from the horror!"

"You know that way to Ost?" Captain Smooth asked, interested in spite of his common sense.

"Oh, yes. Come here and I'll show you."

BEN BRASKEN went to a porthole and pointed through it.

"There," he said. "You can see Ost as plain as can be."

There was nothing when Captain Smooth looked.

"Sure, sure," Captain Smooth said gently. "You just go to sleep and have a rest, and we'll wake you when we anchor at Ost."

He took Ben Brasken's elbow.

Ben Brasken looked at him. He jerked his elbow away.

"Don't act that way!" he shrieked. "You think I'm crazy! You don't believe me! I tell you, I'm as sane as any man on this ship! You've got to go to Ost. They sent me for you. They need help. They've got to have it!"

"Of course, of course," murmured Captain Smooth. "Don't get me wrong, Ben. We'll sail for Ost."

Ben Brasken was not fooled. He became a raving fiend, and tried to get at the gun Captain Smooth kept in his desk.

It took five stout sailors to lash poor Ben Brasken to a stout, padded plank in a spare cabin. Ben Brasken then fainted. He was very weak, and apparently had been without food for days. They noted that his hands were skinned, and thick callouses were on the palms. The palms were also cut and bruised.

Ben Brasken would eat when he regained consciousness. But when they asked him questions, he only glared at them, after saying that what was the use, since they thought him crazy.

When the ship reached San Francisco, they transferred Ben Brasken to the mental ward of a hospital for observation.

Chapter II

THE LADY DIRIGIBLE BUYER

THE strange case of Ben Brasken came to the attention of Doc Savage in the shape of a typewritten report, the first sheet of which was headed:

INCIDENTS POSSIBLY WORTH ATTENTION,
No. 9163. BRASKEN, BEN,
(Sailor who saw phantom city.)

There were a lot of other reports with this one. They covered incidents pretty much all over the world. Some of the reports apparently had no meaning. The premier of an obscure European country had deposited a hundred thousand dollars in his bank account. A famous racketeer had been released from the penitentiary. A scientist had developed an electrical treatment for curing color blindness in the human eye, it was believed.

These reports were made up for Doc Savage by his five aids.

Doc Savage's headquarters occupied the top floor of New York's tallest building. He remained there most of the time, and did not venture out in public, for he had a genuine dislike for being noticed.

It was impossible for him to go about without being noticed. He was a bronze giant who made almost every other man seem small in comparison, although his muscular development was so symmetrical that he did not seem such a giant when standing off by himself. He had straight bronze hair, a little darker than his skin. But his eyes probably made him more striking than any other feature.

They were like pools of flake gold stirred steadily by tiny winds, and they possessed a penetrating, almost hypnotic quality which was quite disturbing, especially to somebody with a guilty conscience.

Doc had been trained from childhood by scientists. He was a scientific product. He had never had a normal youth. The result was that he was an amazing personage. The newspapers called him a mental wizard and a muscular marvel.

Doc Savage read the report about Ben Brasken without showing any emotion.

With Doc in the library of the skyscraper headquarters were two of his aids.

William Harper Littlejohn, more often called "Johnny," had often been described as being two men high and half a man thick. He wore a monocle attached to his lapel. It was really a magnifying glass. Johnny was an eminent archaeologist and geologist. He had one habit which might some day get him slaughtered: He never used a small word when he could think of a big one.

Brigadier General Theodore Marley Brooks was the best-dressed man in America, most persons admitted. He was also a noted lawyer, and carried a harmless-looking black cane that was really a sword cane. Those who knew him very well, or could outrun him, called him "Ham." He did not like the nickname.

Ham had one bad habit: It was Chemistry, his pet. Chemistry was either an ape, chimpanzee, gorilla or baboon, or a mixture. Scientists who tried to figure out just what Chemistry was frequently gave it up and called him the what-is-it.

Doc had just put the Ben Brasken report down and was looking at it when "Monk" came in, looking very excited.

MONK was Lieutenant Colonel Andrew Blodgett Mayfair, chemical wizard, owner of a pet pig called Habeas Corpus. Monk looked almost exactly like Ham's what-is-it, Chemistry, would look like if he weighted two hundred and fifty or so pounds.

Monk was indeed excited. He shifted from one stubby, bowed leg to another.

Ham looked at Monk.

"It must be a woman," Ham said sourly. "Something in skirts is sure to get that freak of nature all worked up. Just anything in skirts will do the trick."

Monk looked at Ham. He looked at Ham as if the latter were a fly some one had missed with the swatter.

"You shyster!" Monk squeaked, in a small child's voice. "Some day I'm gonna cram you all into one shoe!"

Doc asked quietly, "What is it, Monk?"

"A lady to see you," Monk said. "He gazed at the ceiling ecstatically. "And brothers, is she class!"

"I told you so," Ham jeered.

"Show her in," Doc requested.

When the young woman came in, they all got to their feet courteously. But Ham sprang forward and, with great politeness, escorted the young woman to Doc and arranged a chair for her, elbowing aside Monk, who glared indignantly.

No one could recall Monk and Ham ever having treated each other with any civility.

She was sort of a pocket-edition girl. Not that there wasn't enough to her to make a vision who would have disturbed any man's dignity. There definitely was.

Her mink coat was cost and class, and her stockings were so sheer that a second glance was necessary to be sure she wore any. She had large brown eyes, and her hair was about the color of a pecan shell.

She carried her chin in the air, and began to act like a young woman who was accustomed to having men let her have her own way.

"I am Kittrella Merrimore," she said.

Monk and Ham exchanged the kind of glances they might have swapped if they had discovered a harmless-looking butterfly they had been handling was a deadly, venomous moth. They had heard of "Kit" Merrimore. Indeed, she had more money than any young woman should have.

Two jackleg foreign noblemen had sued her in the courts, claiming she had promised to marry them. She had started a transatlantic flight. Her pilot had tried to drown them both by diving into the sea when she refused to wed him at the end of the flight. She was what is known as dynamite.

"You have a small dirigible, I believe," Kit Merrimore told Doc Savage.

The bronze man admitted he did have. If Kit Merrimore was having any effect on him, it failed to show.

"I came to buy your airship," Kit Merrimore stated flatly.

"For what purpose?" Doc Savage inquired.

"You'll pardon me," the lady hell-raiser retorted, "but that happens to be my business."

DOC SAVAGE's three aids waited with great interest for whatever might come.

Doc Savage said nothing after the pretty visitor advised him to keep his nose out of her affairs, which was what it amounted to.

The silence appeared to irk Kit Merrimore. She started tapping the floor angrily with an expensively custom-shod toe.

"Well," she snapped, "how much do you think your airship is worth?"

"It is not for sale," Doc replied quietly.

"Nonsense! Of course it is! How much?"

Doc Savage rested his metallic hands on the desk. The bronze skin on the hands were smooth and fine-grained, and the tendons, when movement caused them to spring out, were hard cables nearly as large as an ordinary man's fingers.

"It seems you do not understand," he said, in a deep, well-controlled voice. "The dirigible is a private craft which we had constructed especially for our own needs. And we would certainly not allow any one to use it without knowing for exactly what purpose it was intended."

Kit Merrimore's toe tapped the floor viciously.

"You talk as if you thought I was going to use it to drop bombs on women and children.

Doc used good judgement. He did not answer this invitation for a quarrel.

The young woman suddenly used a different tack. She had been studying the big bronze man, who was himself far above the average in male pulchritude. Perhaps this had something to do with it. Kit Merrimore smiled sweetly.

"Please," she said, "I really do want the airship badly."

"For what purpose?" Doc asked bluntly.

"I'm truly sorry, but I cannot tell you that," the young lady replied.

"I am equally sorry," Doc said. "You cannot have the airship."

Kit Merrimore's smile would have stopped a war.

"Please," she pleaded.

"You haven't a chance of vamping me into it," Doc said.

Kit Merrimore stamped both feet, and her eyes launched sparks.

"I demand that you sell it to me!" she hissed.

Doc shrugged wearily.

"I'll make you wish you had!" the young woman snapped. "Perhaps you don't know just who I am?"

"You are a young woman who was not spanked often enough when she was little," Doc Savage replied earnestly. "And you have too much money."

Monk and the others held their breath, mortally certain Doc was going to get hit with the first thing the young lady could get her pretty hands on.

Kit Merrimore did grab for a paper weight. Then something happened. She stiffened. She seemed to forget all about Doc and her rage.

Her eyes were fixed on the report about Ben Brasken. She could see Ben Brasken's name. She could also see the notation: "Incidents possibly worth attention," preceding the name.

She moved her brown eyes to Doc Savage. The eyes were wide, amazed, shocked.

"Oh!" she said. "Oh!"

Doc showed no emotion. He hardly ever showed any, for that matter. But his three aids were almost as astonished as the young woman.

Kit Merrimore looked up from the paper.

"So that's it!" she said.

Without another word, she spun and walked out to the place. She seemed in a hurry.

"Monk, Ham," Doc Savage said quietly, "it might be a good idea if you checked up on what she does. Trail her."

Monk and Ham went out.

"I'll be supermalgamated!" said tall, thin Johnny. "An anagrammatical eventuation."

These words were a sample of why a dictionary was necessary to understand Johnny's normal speech. Not for the world would he have stated simply that he was surprised at the puzzling turn events had taken.

KIT MERRIMORE took an express elevator to the street. The express elevators in the building were by no means slow conveyances. Yet Monk and Ham beat her to the street.

They did this by taking Doc's private speed elevator, a lift used only by the bronze man and his aids, and one which would not have been passed by the inspectors for public use simply because it operated at such a speed, that it would have been considered dangerous to individuals with weak physiques.

Monk and Ham hurried out and got in the first taxi they saw. There was a string of cabs at the curb waiting for fares.

There was also an enormous gray town car at the curb. Pedestrians turned around and stared at this car, sometimes running into each other in their absorption. It was a very striking car, streamlined to the last degree.

A round butterball of a Chinaman was behind the wheel, and a lean, dark, very muscular-looking man was in the rear.

Monk and Ham waited.

"There she is," Monk said. "Even if she does expect to be followed, she will never suspect we arrived out in the street before her."

Kit Merrimore got into the aristocratic town car. She was biting her shapely lips in rage.

"Drive up to the park, Two-bit," she told the Celestial. "I want to think."

Then she turned and looked at the dark athlete beside her.

"Lupp, everything went wrong," she said.

"Yes," said the dark "Lupp." "What? Wouldn't he sell us the airship?"

"Worse. He has been investigating that sailor, Ben Brasken. I saw some kind of a report on his desk."

Lupp sat up straight at that. Muscles around his mouth bunched.

"This is a tough break!" he said grimly. "I wonder if he knows the truth?"

"I don't know what he knows. I wasn't fool enough to ask him. What are we going to do?"

"Don't worry, I'll do plenty!" Lupp snapped.

"You had better think twice," the young woman offered. "Doc Savage is not to be taken too lightly. I was very much impressed by him."

"Savage is quite a handsome chap," Lupp said, with a trace of acid.

"Handsome men are a dime a dozen!" retorted Kit Merrimore, who should know. "And furthermore, his looks have nothing to do with it."

"Of course," Lupp agreed dryly.

"Furthermore," snapped Kit Merrimore, "if I should fall in love with Doc Savage or anybody else, it is no concern of yours!"

"Two-bit," the Oriental, said, without turning his head, "It has been said that the mightiest tigers are those whom the jackals follow most."

"What do you mean, you fat heathen?" Kit Merrimore asked.

"Two men," replied Two-bit, "are following us. I have seen them in my rear-view mirror."

Lupp growled, "I'll take care of them mighty quick!"

MONK and Ham sat back in their cab, blissfully unaware that they had been discovered by the sharp-eyed Oriental driver of the town car.

"Lawyers should all be shot," Monk stated firmly. "They're what's wrong with this country."

Ham unsheathed his sword cane and examined a sticky substance on the tip.

"I wonder if this stuff has lost its strength?" he pondered aloud, and looked at Monk speculatively.

The sticky stuff was a drug which produced unconsciousness when the sword cane pricked a victim.

"You stick with that," Monk promised, "and I'll take you by the neck and wind you up like a clock."

They continued the quarrel while their quarry led them into Central Park via the Sixth Avenue entrance. The machine carrying Monk and Ham got up to fifty miles an hour.

Then, for no reason immediately apparent, it rocked wildly, jumped the curb, turned sidewise, went completely over, and lit in about four feet of water which was in a lagoon beside the road. It was very fortunate that the cab had an all-steel body and a good one.

Monk yelled. He always yelled when he got excited. His ordinary voice was that of a child, but his yells were the bellows of a bull.

He kicked about, fought the door. The door was jammed. He batted the glass with a palm. It caved. Monk broke the rest out, and clambered out. He reached back and got Ham by the hair.

"Let's go!" Ham snarled. "I'm not dead yet!"

Monk reached for the driver. At that point, Monk was suddenly conscious of an awful stinging in his eye. They began to water. His nose hurt.

He took a gasping breath, and his lungs and throat began to sting. He bent over in an uncontrollable paroxysm of coughing.

"I'm dyin'!" he croaked.

It was a rather sheepish-looking Monk and Ham who presented themselves at Doc Savage's headquarters. Ham was also mad. His natty morning suit—for which he had just paid the city's most exclusive tailor almost four hundred dollars—had been ruined.

The other two of Doc Savage's little group of five aids were in the skyscraper aerie. They were "Long Tom" and "Renny."

Long Tom was an undersized, pale specimen, such a sickly appearing character indeed that undertakers could not help feeling a wave of prosperity coming when they saw him. He was actually a man who had never been ill. He was an electrical genius. His full name was Major Thomas J. Roberts.

Renny was a big, sour-faced man who led the world

in two things: He was probably the greatest living engineer. And he had bigger fists than any other man. He used them for an aggravating pet diversion of knocking wooden panels out of doors at the most unexpected moments.

"Holy cow!" Renny rumbled, using a voice that was like a lion in a deep cave. "What happened?"

Monk's groan could not have been louder if he had lost an arm.

"Tear gas," he said. "It must have been the kind you squirt out of them little guns that work like fire extinguishers, only you don't pump 'em. Anyway, this dame had her car drive fast, and either she or somebody with her pumped the gas out, and our driver got it and ran off the road into a puddle and turned over."

"And ruined my clothing!" Ham snapped.

"What about the girl?" Doc asked.

"Oh, her?" Monk shrugged. "Search me. They got away."

"They?"

"A Chinaman driving her car. He came the nearest to being a full moon as anybody I ever saw. And there was some kind of a swarthy, athletic-lookin' guy in the car with her. I never saw either him or the Chinaman before."

Doc Savage said nothing more. But he picked up the report on Ben Brasken, tapped it with a metallic forefinger, and glanced at gaunt Johnny.

"A plenary chronographical recapitulation," Johnny said.

"Eh?" Monk said.

"He said that report on Ben Brasken was complete, stupid!" Ham told Monk.

"I wish he'd learn English," Monk growled. "And who are you calling stupid, you mud dauber?"

Doc Savage began to speak without emotion.

"It looks as if this Ben Brasken matter was something that could stand a little of our particular type of attention," he stated. "What do you gentlemen think?"

The expectant grins gave him his answer.

Doc Savage continued. "Your first move might be to

get a line on Kit Merrimore and her two associates, the Chinaman and the dark man. Find out whatever you can. You know the best methods to use. One of you had better remain here to take the reports and assemble them, so that they will be available when I call in."

Monk demanded, "What are *you* going to do?"

Doc did not seem to hear the question.

The bronze man had an aggravating habit of not seeming to hear queries which, for one reason or another, he did not desire to answer. This had a connection with his custom of not letting his aids know what he was doing, frequently, when he worked alone.

The idea was that if one of them should be seized, and perhaps tortured into talking, there would be no information available which would imperil the bronze man or the others.

Renny walked over, calmly drew back, and practically demolished the wooden panel of the library door with one of his huge fists.

"Holy cow!" he said. "This affair kind of interests me already."

He looked very gloomy. It was peculiar with him that he looked the saddest when he was the happiest.

Chapter III

THE SAILOR WHO COULD NOT SWIM

POOR Ben Brasken was still in the wing for mental cases in the San Francisco hospital, and there did not seem to be much chance of his getting out soon.

A number of more or less eminent psychologists, psychopaths, psychophysicists, and a plain M. D. or two had examined Ben Brasken. As was to be expected, they came up with different ideas.

Being puzzled, they expressed themselves with five-dollar words which were not only unintelligible to an average man, but more or less confusing to each other. The truth was that they hadn't been able to quite figure out Ben Brasken.

The hospital was modern, the food good, the nurses easy on the eyes, and the patients had the use of a croquet court, swimming pool, short golf course—all surrounded by a high man-tight, woven-wire fence—so there was no reason why a poor sailor man with nowhere else to go should want to leave.

Ben Brasken seemed to have resigned himself. He sat in his chair on the lawn beside the swimming pool, his favorite spot, most of the time. It was as if, being a seafaring man, he liked to be near a bit of water.

It was there that Ben Brasken received the large, swarthy sailor who came to visit him. At least, the big visitor had a little white sailor hat perched on the back of his thatch of dark, curly hair.

There was one striking thing in particular about the visitor: He had one bad eye. It looked exactly like a large pigeon egg, pink and quite awful. The other eye was protected by a pair of colored spectacles which were minus the lens over the bad eye.

"Hello, Ben, you old swab," said the visitor, when the nurse brought him up.

The nurse, convinced he knew Ben Brasken, departed.

Ben Brasken then muttered, "Look here, I don't know you!"

"Sure you don't," said the other, and took a seat

cross-legged on the edge of the swimming pool beside which Ben Brasken's chair was situated. "I wanted to talk to you."

"Whatcha want?"

"Look here," grunted the other. "Suppose I knew a sailor, and he was on a boat makin' the run from Frisco to Melbourne, and he reached Frisco one time and talked some when he was drunk about seein' a town of some kind in the ocean. Mind you, the town wasn't there. Then, on the next voyage, supposin' he disappeared off the ship."

"Why are you interested?"

"Supposin' this other sailor was my brother."

"I ain't your brother! I ain't got a brother."

"Nobody said you were or had."

"Oh!" Ben Brasken thought that over. "You mean that you had a brother and that's what happened to 'im?"

"Maybe."

"You got a heck of a hindforemost way of sayin' so."

The other shrugged. "Did you see any sign of my brother?"

Ben Brasken leaned forward eagerly. "Say, do you really believe I'm not crazy?"

"Maybe my brother wasn't crazy," the other said.

"What was his name?"

"Gulliver Smith."

"I didn't see him," sighed Ben Brasken. "The only white people I saw were the man named Martin Space and the woman."

BEN BRASKEN had been under an intense strain for days. He had known he was considered insane, and that was enough to worry any man. Now that he had a chance to talk, he literally overflowed conversation. deed, the guest's very ugliness was something that in-spite of the latter's undeniably hideous appearance. In-deed, the guests' very ugliness was something that in-spired pity, and therefore a certain amount of kindness.

The story Ben Brasken told was almost word for word the same one he had told Captain Smooth, the hard-boiled master of the ancient hooker *Benny Boston*. When he came to the mention of the "great horror" he had seen, he did not go deeper into details than that.

"Hold on!" interjected the visitor. "What was this horror?"

Ben Brasken leaned back and closed his eyes. He seemed to be thinking. He shuddered.

"To tell the truth, that is what is worrying me," he said. "The strain of that long swim back from Ost carrying the two iron keys must have been too much for me. The doctors here said I was nearly dead from exhaustion and lack of food.

"I swam for many, many hours. It must have dulled my mind, or something. A lot of details are faint. I can't tell exactly what the horror was."

"Think hard."

"I have. For days. But if anything, it all seems to grow more vague, like a bad dream. I told that to those psychowhatchacall'ems who examined me. They didn't seem to know what to think."

"That's too bad," muttered the visitor.

"It was something terrible, this horror," Ben Brasken said. "But I can't remember. I guess I am going bats maybe."

"Don't let 'em kid you!" snorted the other. "Listen, my boat sank one time and I was out in an open dory for three weeks without food and with only a little water, and I'm tellin' you for a long time I couldn't remember a thing that happened to me."

Ben Brasken grinned. "I'm sure glad to hear you say that. Everybody thinks I'm nuts."

"Forget it!" chuckled the one-eyed guest. "Look, what about that iron key you mentioned?"

"I used them to get in and out of Ost." Ben Brasken pinched his eyes shut and puckered his brows in deep thought. "Oh, damn the luck! I can't remember. It's all so hazy. Like if I was drunk the whole time. Only I wasn't. I never drink."

"You had two of them?"

"Oh, yes. One for each hand."

"But when you reached the ship, you only had one."

"Darn, that's right." Ben Brasken shut his eyes again. "Well, I must have lost the other one while I was swimming. It was pretty heavy."

"You swam and carried these two pieces of iron?"

"Oh, yes."

The visitor now arose, as if to depart. But the big, one-eyed fellow seemed to have become stiff while seated cross-legged on the edge of the pool. He staggered wildly, his legs not tracking. To keep from falling, he grabbed Ben Brasken's chair.

Ben Brasken, chair and all, toppled into the swimming pool.

BEN BRASKEN landed in the water with a splash. The pool was deep at this point, almost ten feet. The chair was of metal and sank. Ben Brasken also went down, but came to the top, splashing and gagging.

"Help!" he croaked.

Then he sank again.

The pool was very clear. Every move poor Ben Brasken made in his wild struggles could be seen plainly. He had both his eyes and mouth wide open, and big bubbles kept coming out of his mouth and nose.

He grabbed frantically, again and again, for the surface. He did manage to reach the top, but went down again. When he was momentarily on the surface, he emitted a piteous shriek.

Hospital attendants had by now reached the pool. Two of them sprang in. Ben Brasken grabbed them as a drowning man will, and there was quite a turmoil until every one was hauled out of the pool.

The big, dark, one-eyed sailor started walking away.

"Hey, you!" an attendant said sharply. "I'm not sure, but it looked as if you pushed Brasken into the pool."

The one-eyed man said nothing, but walked faster.

The hospital attendants were accustomed to handling persons who did the unexpected. They pursued the big, dark visitor. A whistle blew. More attendants appeared. Burly fellows, strong men who knew how to control maniacs with the greatest of facility.

They closed in on the big, dark one. Two attendants reached for his arms. They reached confidently, for the big Cyclops was merely walking along. But they got a shock. Their hands got only empty air.

The one-eyed man had not dodged, apparently. They grabbed for him again. Once more, the incredible happened. The truth dawned on them. Their quarry was as fast as the proverbial greased lightning.

A wild mêlée followed. Men rushed the dark visitor from all directions. He whipped about in a fashion that was astonishing. Reaching a door, he dodged through. A nurse cried out his location. When the attendants reached there, the fellow was gone. They looked about wildly for him.

A few moments later the dark, one-eyed mariner dropped from a window of the hospital and sauntered away, unobserved.

Back in the hospital grounds, attendants stood around Ben Brasken, who was little the worse for his immersion.

Ben Brasken's ducking had proved one thing: He could not swim a stroke.

Chapter IV

THE HIDING PLACE

THE big, dark sailor with the pigeon-egg eye next turned up in the vicinity of the steamship pier to which the ancient hooker *Benny Boston* was tied.

It was dusk when he arrived. There was only one gangplank down, and a sailor loafed at this to keep just anybody from wandering aboard, a precaution against sneak thieves.

The sailor applied a match to a cigarette, and it was dark enough for the match flame to blind him slightly. When he had accustomed his eyes by blinking, he discovered the Cyclops sailor in front of him.

"Hy'ah, captain," said the latter.

Around the water, every one calls every one else a captain, whether the title is warranted or not. Just as all elderly gentlemen are called colonel in Kentucky.

"Greetings," said the sailor.

"When you sailin'?" asked pigeon-egg-eyed man.

"Couple of days."

"Got a full crew?"

"Dunno. You better see the Old Man. Cap'n Smooth. He's not aboard to-night."

"Thanks, captain," said the one-eyed sailor. He walked away, and was swallowed in the darkness. He had gone in the direction of town.

His course did not take him toward town for any considerable distance, however. He doubled back and went directly to one of the big hawsers by which the *Benny Boston* was tied to the pier. He seemed to be the brother of a cat in his ability to get about in the dark.

Without seeming to exert his muscles in the least, he swung along the hawser. He passed the big conical tin rat guard through which the hawser ran, and went on.

The rat guard was turned so as to keep the rats on shore, but it would have been more appropriate the other way, rats being much more plentiful on the old steamer than on shore.

Once on deck, the prowler entered the holds. He showed an extraordinary familiarity with the interior of

24

freight steamers on ancient vintage. He lighted his way with a flashlight, which emitted only a small streak of light.

He began searching the ship. A thorough job, he did; but he seemed little interested in the holds, passages and cabins which were used most frequently.

Nothing did he miss, which was unusual, because there were numerous crannies of the most remote kind. The prowler even raised a trapdoor and wormed down into the bilge, wading around in water which was incredibly smelly and coated with almost a quarter of an inch of grease and scum.

He was very secretive. Since it was early in the night, sailors were still moving about, those who had not gone ashore. The searcher dodged these expertly. Altogether, he was quiet enough to have done a first-class spook job in haunting a house.

In a little-used compartment back of the anchor chain locker near the bow of the boat, he came across something that seemed to interest him. The niche was a gloomy one, closed by a hatch, and apparently not used at all.

The place was littered with empty cans. The searcher examined the cans closely. Tomatoes, corn, beans, mostly. Most of them bore grimy finger prints.

Some of the cans had been opened only a few days ago. Others had been emptied less recently. This difference, while it was not quite as plain as print, could be discerned by close inspection.

It was evident that some one had lived in the cubicle, eating out of the cans for an interval that might have been three weeks.

There were certain other signs to indicate whoever this was had been completely a hermit, had not left the place at all.

Judging from the signs, the hermit had entered the place about a month previously and had remained there until about a week ago.

This was the period during which Ben Brasken had been missing.

THE dark, one-eyed giant now produced two articles from his pockets. One item was a pocket finger-print set, such as police detectives sometimes carry. The other object was a copy, or rather the page itself, from the hospital records made out when Ben Brasken was committed. It bore Ben Brasken's finger prints.

A few seconds, and the mysterious sailor was comparing the finger prints on the emptied food cans with those of Ben Brasken.

They were the same. Ben Brasken, then, had been the hermit.

The food cans were not the only interesting objects. In moving them aside—there was rather a litter of them—the hunter found four steel hacksaw blades, two files, a brace containing a metal-boring bit, and two or three bolts. There was also a slab of rusty iron, three inches or so thick, more than a foot wide, and a little longer than wide.

The hacksaw blade teeth were almost worn away, the two files had seen much service, and the bit's cutting edges were chipped and rounded. Rectangular pieces had been sawed out of the iron. Two of them.

Under a pile of tin cans was an oblong iron block equipped with a handle, an exact duplicate of the block Ben Brasken had been carrying when they found him apparently climbing aboard the *Benny Boston*. The key, he had called it.

It would seem that the blocks had been made here. And Ben Brasken had spent the time on the job which he claimed he had expended in visiting Ost.

The big, one-eyed prowler seemed satisfied with what had been found, but was thorough enough to go over the rest of the old steamer. He did not devote much time to anything else that he found.

He carried the flatiron-shaped block equipped with a handle when he went on deck.

It was fabulously dark outside, almost as black as it had been in the smelly innards of the ship. The big hunter moved with feline quiet toward the hawser by which he had come aboard.

Out on the bay, a pair of tugs began blasting their whistles at each other. The echoes bounced back from warehouses and buildings until there was a gobbling uproar.

This accounted for the piegon-egg eyed sailor bumping into another prowler on deck before he discovered his presence.

There was no preliminary word exchanged. The other maurauder hit the big sailor with a fist. The fist hit the large one's chest with a sound as if a big jungle drum had been thumped.

The two sprang upon each other. Both seemed fully confident of an immediate victory. They strained, grunted, and clothing tore. They tripped, went to the deck.

Their fighting styles were vastly different. The big, dark fellow used fist science. The other felt about with snaky fingers, twisting a joint here, punching a nerve center there. Jujutsu. Skilled, too.

Suddenly, the giant with the pigeon-egg eye commenced to demonstrate that he also knew jujutsu. He was, indeed, the other's master at the tricky joint-cracking, nerve-punishing science. His foe emitted a sudden squall of pain, after which he could barely move.

The beam of the big sailor's flashlight licked over the gasping assailant.

The fellow was a rather large and almost round Chinaman who was about the color of homemade butter.

Had Doc Savage's two aids been present, they would have recognized him as the same Celestial who had driven pretty Kit Merrimore's town car in New York City.

A sharp shout came from amidships. Running feet pounded. The fight had drawn attention.

Chapter V

THE PHANTOM CELESTIAL

THE globular Oriental had the cunning of his race. He lay quiet until he had enough strength to emit a yell that would have raised the dead.

"He tly kill me!" he squawled. "Help poor Chinaman!"

The footsteps approached with the rattle of a hailstorm coming across a tin roof. The crew of the *Benny Boston*. Some of them had hurricane lanterns.

They did the natural thing. They decided to grab both strangers and ask questions afterward. The Chinaman was a stranger, certain enough.

"Who's the laundryman?" a sailor barked, and that proved that.

The dark giant with the strange eye tried to pick the Oriental up and get over the side with him, but the Celestial kicked and used his hands. He was really a master of his jujutsu. He managed to delay the business of carrying him away.

Two sailors leaped upon the dark marauder. They were promptly flung backward.

The Oriental sank to the deck and moaned, "He fella bleak mine leg!"

It was clever strategy. The sailors gave him no attention, but flocked upon the big, dark fellow. As soon as no one was looking at him, the Celestial bobbed up and disappeared down the hawser to the gloomy shore.

The *Benny Boston* sailors were tough lads who knew all about fighting, or thought they did. After they had been mixing with the big, dark fellow for a few seconds, they began to conclude there were things they didn't know.

Men suddenly found themselves on deck, paralyzed, and not knowing in the least just what had happened to them. Those who got hold of the foe frequently thought some one had introduced iron bars the size of arms and legs in the fight.

The hurricane lanterns became smashed, one by

one, and the mêlée went on in the darkness. Captain Smooth came running from his cabin, carrying a long, heavy boat hook. With this shillalah, he poked and whacked, until someone kicked most of the skin off his right shin.

The fight became less violent. One man scrambled clear, struck several matches and managed to relight what was left of one of the hurricane lanterns.

They saw then why the fight was less violent. They were only scrapping each other. Their foe, the big tartar with the queer eye, had faded away, probably overboard.

Captain Smooth hopped around on one foot, nursing his peeled shin, and began to say things which, remarkably it seemed, did not melt the surrounding ironwork.

One sailor backed hastily to the rear of the group and examined the toe of his shoe. He hurriedly brushed off some bunches of the skipper's hide which were sticking to the toe. The hide somewhat resembled the kind of ostrich leather they make purses out of.

THE big, dark, strange-eyed sailor was not only ashore; he had reached the street which ran beyond the piers. A small coupé was a hundred yards away, and still gathering speed.

It is, of course, impossible for a man to outrun any respectable kind of an automobile in a test of speed, but the big sailor very nearly succeeded.

The Celestial in the car saw him barely in time, stepped on the gas, and got away. The car motor had a carbon knock, but that didn't hurt.

The big, dark sailor stopped. He had just covered two hundred yards at a clip that would have taken the breath of a professional sprint timer. Yet his breath was not coming with undue speed.

He went back to the pier, listened, learned the sailors off the *Benny Boston* were ashore searching. He paid no attention, but entered the pier shed silently. Once, he could have reached out and taken the cigarette off the lips of a searching *Benny Boston* deckhand.

The dark sailor got the flatiron-shaped piece of steel

with the attached handle which he had found in the cubicle aboard the ship. Because of its weight, he had left this behind while pursuing the rotund Oriental.

The big, dark, strange-eyed sailor left the vicinity with ghostly stealth.

One of the city's more obscure hotels saw him next. He seemed to have a room there. He entered it, closed the door, pulled the shade, listened for a while to make sure no one was listening, then went to the bureau mirror.

With a tiny suction cup gripping device that somewhat resembled the rubber part of an eye dropper, the sailor proceeded to remove colored glass caps which fitted over his eyeballs, under the lids. These were transparent enough to permit vision through them. One had given him the pigeon-eye.

A pastelike chemical and an application of friction and soapsuds took the curl out of his hair. The hair became gray, almost white when the chemical treatment was done.

A small trunk yielded a dignified and very conservative business suit, also an excellently made mustache and Vandyke beard, spectacles with a black ribbon, and a case of instruments such as surgeons carry. There was also a case of business cards.

Another pair of the glass eyeballs caps disguised his eyes, and a few drops of a chemical made them watery and old-looking.

The surprising individual walked out of the hotel as an elderly, dignified gentleman. The iron block was in his surgical bag.

He turned up at the hospital where Ben Brasken was confined and presented one of his cards in the office.

The card said:

Kurt Von Vallenstadt

Psychiatrist   Vienna, Berlin.

"*Ja*," said the old gentleman, using a grand manner. "Vass it possible for me to examine dot sailor Ben Brasken?"

"It is rather late, doctor," he was told.

"*Ja.* I know dot. But mine plane leave for New York very early in morning. Dot Ben Brasken case interest me very mooch."

After some hesitation, he was told he might see Ben Brasken.

Ben Brasken occupied a ward in which there were three other beds, but the other three were empty. Ben Brasken was reading a detective magazine. He lowered the magazine.

Ben Brasken's forehead was covered almost to the eyes by a damp towel, and the sheet was pulled up over his chin.

The nurse departed.

"What do you want?" Ben Brasken asked hoarsely.

THE old gentleman put the bag on the table. "I have something to show you."

He took out the flatiron object.

"Huh?" said Ben Brasken.

"This is a duplicate of the key you had when they found you climbing aboard the *Benny Boston,* apparently," stated the visitor.

"Oh." Ben Brasken blinked dark eyes.

"I found it in a small, unused cubbyhole near the bow of the *Benny Boston.* It had been made in that cubby. There were some other things in the place which proved you were hiding out there during the time you claim you visited this place called Ost."

"Who are you, feller?"

For answer, the old fellow handed over one of his cards. The hand which came out from under the bed covers and took it was hairy, brown and rather thick.

"Yah," he said, after glancing at the card. "A pill-pusher, eh?"

"You are not insane," said the visitor.

"Thanks."

"You are a skillful liar."

"I may be a sick man, but don't get too tough with me, you old goat!"

"What is behind this?"

This got no answer.

"Der jig is up, *ja,* stated the elderly man. "You had best talk."

"You want the dirt, sawbones?"

"Der truth, *ja.*"

The man on the bed grinned. "I wanted to get my name in the newspapers."

"Ach!"

"Sure. All my life, nobody had ever noticed me. So I got an idea, see. I had some money saved up."

"Vot has der money saved got to do mit it?"

"Shut up and you'll see. I used the money to buy one of them high-powered magic lanterns that they use to throw pictures on clouds for advertising. I took a slide of a view of lower Manhattan Island, sandpapered off some of the paint on it so it would look spooky, and threw it on a cloud.

"I pointed the machine through a porthole in the hull of the ship, see. Nobody got wise. They saw this thing on the clouds. That was the mysterious city them fool sailors thought they saw."

"Ja! Amazing!"

"Sure it was, you old nanny. Then I disappeared into the hold, made them iron things, and one night went on deck, waited until I heard a sailor coming, then slid down the rope and got wet, then climbed back and they all thought I was just coming aboard. Nobody would see through that, eh?"

"Nein. Nobody vould."

"I told a string of lies about a visit to a city called Ost."

"Ja, but suppose somebody questioned your ability to swim mit dot iron you were carrying?"

"That's why I left the one behind. I could swim with one, all right."

"Maybe you could," the visitor said grimly, "but Ben Brasken could not swim."

"Huh?"

"You are not Ben Brasken."

Chapter VI

THE NEW BEN BRASKEN

THE man on the bed really bore only a vague facial resemblance to Ben Brasken. He was almost a foot taller and nearly a hundred pounds heavier.

His hand came out from under the covers. It held a gun.

"Hold everything!" he gritted.

The bearded old gentleman sat very quiet.

"I ain't Ben Brasken, all right!" snarled the man with the gun. "I'm a pal of Ben's. Two or three of Ben's pals got tired of them keepin' 'im in here and makin' out he was a nut, so we took 'im out. I stayed here so that Ben would have time to get clear. Anybody lookin' in would take it for granted that I was Ben."

"And dot story about der magic lantern?" the elderly visitor asked thoughtfully.

"That was straight. It was just a stunt of Ben's. Poor little feller. He didn't know they would put him in the birdhouse."

The man untangled himself from the bed covers and stood erect. He was very muscular, dark, and had a not unhandsome, if rather hard, face.

"Two-bit!" he called softly.

"Allee same on deck, Mis' Lupp," said a perfectly round and big Oriental, hauling himself in through the window, outside which he must have been crouching.

"You rice-eating ape!" said dark, athletic Lupp. "You called out my name!"

"You do same to me," reminded the big Celestial.

Lupp looked angry, but motioned. "Tie up whiskers here, and we'll blow. Our gag didn't go off so good."

The Oriental advanced, picked off a bedsheet, rolled it and made a rope. He evidently did not go to the movies, or he would have made the mistake of tearing the sheet to make it into ropes. A sheet that is torn is much more easily parted.

He came close to the bearded old gentleman, stopped, bent forward, and his slant eyes popped in astonishment.

"This lowly one has many times wondered how Little Led Liding Hood felt when she find wolf in little sheep's clothing," he said.

"What's wrong, you yellow peril?" Lupp growled. "You've got the story cockeyed, anyhow. Red Riding Hood's grandma was the one the wolf pre——"

"This fella all same on *Benny Boston*," interjected Two-bit.

"What?"

"He fella me tell 'bout. Only now he all same whiskel false!"

Lupp sprang forward with an oath, gritted, "I'll see how false the whiskers are!" and grabbed the whiskers and yanked.

Results were not quite as expected. The whiskers came off readily enough. But Lupp cried out, dropped them with wild haste, and ogled his palm.

A small puncture in his palm oozed a drop of crimson.

"There's a needle or something in them whiskers!" he snarled. "It stuck me! It felt like a spring or something made it drive into my hand!"

"That velly stlange," said Two-bit wonderingly.

"Yeah—yeah——"

Lupp drew in a full breath, shut his eyes and fell heavily on his face.

Two-bit, the fat Oriental, had nothing wrong with what is technically called reactions. He whirled, and seemed to be in the air before he was halfway around.

His gigantic leap took him to the window. He sailed through it, headfirst.

The big man who had pretended to be a foreign psychiatrist was only a jump behind. He reached the window, looked out. He ducked back with great haste.

Lightning struck three times outside the window, if noise was any indication. Two-bit's gun was evidently of enormous caliber. Bullets gouged plaster off the ceiling. A patient upstairs emitted an unearthly yell, which was promptly echoed by howls and screams all over the hospital. Two demented persons began to laugh like hyenas.

The big man inside the hospital room seized the mirror which lay on a table, and used it to examine the vicinity outside the window.

But Two-bit was gone by now.

Whipping back to Lupp, the big man picked the unconscious fellow up, went to the window, dropped through, and glided into the handiest patch of darkness.

Over to the right, there was a series of metallic squeaking sounds, then half a dozen sharp twangs. Some one was cutting the wire fence around the rear of the hospital, using a stout cutter, no doubt.

The big man made for the sounds.

Long before he reached them, he heard a low gasp, a squawky Oriental curse, and a blow that was louder than either gasp or curse.

The big man quickened his pace. He heard an automobile engine start, race, and connect with rear wheels with a mighty gear clash. The car left. Its engine had a carbon knock which did not seem to slow it up much.

There was a hole in the high wire fence. The big man boosted the senseless Lupp through—Lupp was still breathing—and followed. It was very dark. He took five paces and his toe touched something that yielded.

The flashlight he had used on the *Benny Boston,* the one which emitted a white splinter, came into use.

The man on the ground was much taller than necessary, and thinner than it seemed any individual could be and still stay out of a coffin. It was not necessary to pick up his wrist to find a pulse. The regular puffing of the artery in his wrist was visible.

The man on the ground was the eminent archaeologist, geologist and Doc Savage aid, William Harper Littlejohn.

The big man carried both Johnny and Lupp and left the vicinity.

After a while, Johnny revived enough to say, "I'll be superamalgamated!"

Chapter VII

THE BRONZE MAN

JOHNNY let the exclamation, his favorite and the one he used on all possible occasions, suffice until he had gotten his head cleared. Then he did some thinking. The cogitation led him to making a mistake, as it sometimes does.

He hauled off and tried to knock the big man carrying him senseless. He did not quite succeed. But he did cause the big fellow to fall down with his double burden.

"Johnny!" said the big man reproachfully.

"Doc Savage!" Johnny exploded.

"Yes," said the remarkable individual who had been first a pigeon-eyed sailor, then an eminent psychiatrist from Vienna and Berlin.

"An indefeasible eventuation—I mean, I didn't know it was you!" Johnny gulped.

Johnny was addicted to his amazing words on most occasions, but when he was alone with Doc Savage, he did not use them.

For Johnny, it was a marked token of respect to the bronze man, or possibly he was afraid of misusing some of his tongue-twisters, which it was to be suspected he did occasionally, although no one had ever caught him.

"What happened?" Doc Savage queried.

"Well," Johnny said dizzily, "you disguised yourself as a sailor this afternoon and entered the hospital to talk to Ben Brasken. You left Long Tom, Renny and myself posted around the hospital grounds to watch for anything suspicious. Then——"

"With a reference to a moment ago," Doc put in. "What occurred?"

"I heard somebody cutting the wires of that fence, ran to the spot, and got the most beautiful knock on the head I ever received," Johnny said.

"You feel all right?"

"Not all right. Not by a long shot. But I think I'll live."

"Can you walk?"

"I might run if I had to," Johnny admitted.

They walked quickly through the gloomy streets, Doc Savage carrying Lupp.

Johnny had a flashlight on his person. He turned it on Lupp.

"I'll be superamalgamated!" he exclaimed. "His connaturalness of physiognomy—I mean, he is the guy Monk and Ham described as being in the car with the Oriental and Kit Merrimore in New York!"

"Yes," Doc Savage agreed. "And the Oriental was the same one who just knocked you out."

"Ouch!" Johnny felt the back of his head where he had been struck. "What does it all mean?"

"Ben Brasken is evidently the key," Doc Savage said. "They carried him off to get him in a spot where he would not be questioned, is my guess."

"You think Ben Brasken could tell us what all the shooting is about?"

"An examination of him might be of assistance, would be a more accurate way of putting it."

"Well, we should not have much trouble finding him," said Johnny.

The gaunt geologist had been a little flippant for a few moments, which was vastly unlike his usual self. It must have been some after effect of the blow, or perhaps his real nature had loosened up for a moment and asserted itself. At any rate, he was getting his dignity back now.

"What do you mean 'no trouble finding Ben Brasken'?" Doc queried.

"Long Tom and Renny were left at the hospital with myself," Johnny said.

"Of course."

"Well, we saw them carry off Ben Brasken. Long Tom and Renny followed them. They should find where Brasken was taken."

Doc and Johnny reached a car. This was a rented machine which Doc Savage had secured for their use. The bronze man drove, heading for his hotel.

Johnny seemed to have a headache by now. He held

his rather large cranium and muttered. "It would seem that our elaborate precautions to let no one know we were coming to San Francisco, as well as your entering the hospital in disguise, were wasted."

Doc reminded, "The disguise was largely to avoid public attention and newspaper notice. Too much publicity for us would not only point out to any possible enemies what we were doing, but it would draw down a swarm of well-meaning amateur detectives which would hamper us."

"Circumstantiality indistinguishable—er—to say nothing of the flood of imaginary and worthless clues which would descend upon us," Johnny said.

The fake Ben Brasken—Lupp, if that was his name —stirred feebly.

"He seems to be drugged," Johnny remarked. "How did it happen?"

By the time Doc Savage had explained the needle in the beard, and touched briefly on the fundamental urge which seems to dwell within every human being to grab the whiskers of a foe, immediately he gets in a fight with one, they had reached the hotel.

"Women apparently are driven irresistibly to seize hair when in a conflict," Doc expounded. "A beard seems to offer the same temptation to a man."

They drove into an alley at the rear of the hotel. From this, access could be had to the freight elevator without disturbing the hotel guests. The elevator operator looked deaf, dumb and blind as he took them up.

Johnny spoke when they were carrying Lupp down the corridor to Doc's room.

"Long Tom and Johnny were going to report to the hotel here when they found where Ben Brasken was taken," he said. "But I wonder if it was the best idea to let them take Ben Brasken away?"

"By trailing these men who seized Ben Brasken, we may be able to find their headquarters, and by eavesdropping or planting hidden microphones, learn what is back of this excitement," Doc explained.

Johnny nodded. "I hope Long Tom or Johnny has reported. If they have, it will be attached to that photographic recording device we left in the room, hooked to the telephone."

They reached their room.

Doc and Johnny entered with their captive.

Pale, undersized Long Tom and big-fisted Renny stood in the room. Long Tom looked gloomy. Renny looked moderately cheerful, which was bad, considering that the better things went, the more gloom he would register.

"I'll be superamalgamated!" Johnny exploded. "Why aren't you two trailing the gang who got Ben Brasken?"

Long Tom took in a long draft of air.

"They gave us the slip," he imparted.

Doc Savage placed Lupp in a chair, got handcuffs out of a metal box which held innumerable other gadgets, and handcuffed him to the chair. Then he administered a chemical to the man with a hypodermic needle.

"A stimulant," the bronze man explained. "It will cause him to revive in a few minutes."

Johnny frowned grimly at Lupp. "If we fail to make him talk, it looks as if we were going to be out on a limb without any information."

This caused big-fisted Renny to emit a rumble of self-disgust.

"We got a bad break trailing those fellows," he said. "They crossed a street, and an instant later, a string of fire trucks came down the street, and we couldn't possible cut through."

Doc Savage said, "We had better get set before Lupp regains consciousness. Johnny, you are something of psychologist, so your job will be to sit out here and watch Lupp while we try our trick."

"What trick?"

Doc glanced at Lupp, who was showing signs of awakening.

"No time to explain," the bronze man decided. "Just watch him, Johnny."

Johnny took a seat in a secluded corner, picked up a newspaper and arranged it so he could pretend to read it, but really watch Lupp.

Doc, Long Tom and Renny entered the adjacent room. They had, as a matter of fact, taken the entire floor of the hotel. They closed the door.

Johnny continued to pretend to read the newspaper, and watched Lupp. In a few moments, Lupp opened his eyes and looked around. Johnny made a show of not noticing.

From the next room came what sounded like Ben Brasken's rather whining voice.

"I tell yuh, I'm scared to talk!" he said.

Doc Savage's trained, deep tone said, "What would you say if that Oriental, Two-bit, had told us the whole story?"

At this, Johnny saw Lupp give a distinct start.

Johnny kept his bony face expressionless. Doc Savage was in the other room, imitating Ben Brasken's voice, and making conversation of a nature intended to soften Lupp up for the questioning.

Ben Brasken's faked voice said, "Two-bit didn't lay nothin' onto me!"

"No," Doc Savage said quietly, "but Two-bit is going to be the cause of things becoming tough for Lupp, as well as the girl, Kit Merrimore."

"Two-bit laid it onto them?"

"Yes. Possibly he was passing the buck, though."

Lupp's face was twisted with astonishment and uneasiness. He was deceived.

The voices went on:

Ben Brasken: "What's Lupp supposed to have done?"

Doc: "Plenty. What would you say if you were told Two-bit claimed Lupp shot a hospital attendant during the excitement. That sounds like murder, eh?"

Ben Brasken: "Whew! Then they'll hang Lupp!"

Doc: "Possibly."

Brasken: "Maybe they can't prove it."

Doc: "If Two-bit testified that Lupp murdered the man, they would."

Brasken: "Gimme a minute to think, and I'll tell you all I can."

Doc: "Very well. In the meantime. I'll see what Lupp has to say, if he is awake."

DOC appeared in the door, glanced at Lupp, seemed surprised to find him conscious.

"Ready to talk?" Doc asked.

"Go to the devil!" Lupp snarled.

Doc said wearily, "Johnny, you might as well call the police."

Johnny strode to the telephone.

"Wait a minute!" Lupp exploded. "What're you tryin' to pull on me here?"

Doc Savage said quietly, "It is very simple. "Listen."

The bronze man went back to the connecting door, opened it and leaned through.

"Two-bit," he said, "are you still sure Lupp murdered that hospital attendant when he was trying to escape?"

"Me fella velly celtain," replied a voice that would hardly be taken for any but Two-bit's.

From where he sat, Lupp could not see the bronze man imitate the voice.

"Damn!" Lupp groaned. "Look here! How about us making a deal?"

"What kind?" Doc queried, turning.

"You turn me loose," Lupp countered, "and I'll let you in on the biggest thing you ever——"

At least four bullets came crashing through the door.

Chapter VIII

MURDER VICTIM

THE unexpected, even at its mildest, is startling. A man who almost steps on a mouse may jump only a little less mildly than if he had stepped on a jungle lion.

Johnny leaped as high as his chair. When he came down, he had in one hand a weapon which resembled an oversized automatic pistol, but which was really a supermachine pistol of Doc's development. A Western bad man of the '80s could not have drawn his shooting iron quicker.

Lupp yelled, "I'm in the center of the room, guys! Be careful!"

Johnny leaped to the door into the inner room, waited there, his machine pistol ready. He seemed surprised when Doc Savage shoved him on into the room with Long Tom and Renny and slammed the door.

Lupp was now shut off from them in the next room. And the guns were crashing in the corridor. Blasting the lock out, no doubt.

Johnny exploded, "But, Doc! When they came through the door, with this pistol and mercy bullets, I can——"

"You might," Doc Savage said quietly. "But that would not find Ben Brasken."

"Oh," Johnny said, understanding.

"Keep them from getting in here," Doc warned.

Renny and Long Tom had likewise produced machine pistols.

"Fat chance!" Renny rumbled.

The shooting in the other room abruptly ceased. The men in the hallway kicked the door in.

The round Oriental, Two-bit, led the raiders. His associates were tough-looking fellows.

THEY ran to Lupp. Since he was handcuffed to the chair, and the chair was stout, they could not get him loose. They picked him up chair and all.

"Get Ben Brasken!" Lupp yelled. "He's in the next room!"

"That Doc Savage fella tell you stoly," explained Two-bit.

"What?"

"We still got Ben Brasken."

Lupp understood then that he had been tricked. He was too shocked to get mad.

"Beat it!" he ordered.

Two-bit and the others showed willingness to do that. They carried Lupp and the chair into the hall, popped into the elevator. The elevator operator sat in one corner of the cage, mouth open, jaw skinned, breathing.

The cage went down.

"How'd you find me?" Lupp wanted to know.

"Velly simple." Two-bit shook his shoulders. "Me lait till men take you away. I follow."

"Oh." Lupp grimaced. "Damn Savage anyhow. But he still don't know what it's all about yet."

Two-bit looked as calm as ever. "We listen," he sing-songed. "We note stlange words coming from you."

Lupp swore and looked fierce. "Don't get the wrong idea, pigtail! I was getting ready to save my neck, maybe set a trap for Savage. I thought he had you and Ben Brasken, and that you talked."

After that there was silence.

The cage reached the lobby. Several persons were staring curiously, and there was a crowd of small proportions out in the street. The shots upstairs, of course, had been heard.

The raiders calmly shot part of the bulbs out of the chandeliers, shot some of the glass out of the front windows, and the spectators all used good judgment: They dived into the handiest shelter.

Two-bit and the others carried Lupp to two cars parked on the street. They divided their number between the machines, and the cars got going.

A police siren was howling in the distance.

Big-fisted Renny, leaning out of a hotel window, heard the siren. From the window, he could not see the street, but he could hear the cars going away.

On the inner side of the window sill was a deep nick. The tine of a grappling hook had made it. To the end of the grapple was attached a long, thin very stout silk line. Doc Savage had gone down this.

Renny squinted into the darkness. He could not see Doc. For that matter, the bronze man had been gone for some moments.

Renny snorted and went out to make explanations to the police, who had by now arrived. This would not be too difficult. Doc Savage and his men held a special commission from the California governor designating them as special investigators with police authority, which took in a lot of territory.

Long Tom, the electrical wizard, opened a metal case—Doc Savage's equipment was transported in metal containers which looked very much alike except for painted numbers—and brought out a short-wave radio transmitting and receiving apparatus. The antenna which this used was hardly larger than a walking stick, and telescoped. He switched it on, adjusted the dials, and left it on.

Soft crackles of static and nothing else came from the loud-speaker for almost half an hour.

"Long Tom," Doc Savage's voice said from the speaker.

"Coast Avenue and Tuna Street," the bronze man said, when Long Tom answered. "Better hurry."

COAST AVENUE meant water-front dives. Tuna Street was wholesale fish. There was plenty of darkness. The wad of clouds above had started leaking fine rain.

Johnny stood in a dark alley and jumped a foot at least when Doc Savage spoke beside him.

"The pier to which the *Benny Boston* is tied is at the end of this street," Doc Savage said. "The trail led to a waterfront rooming house near by. The proprietor of the rooming house advised me, when he was questioned, that a man answering the description of Ben Brasken had taken a room, along with some other men."

"We're gettin' close to the end of the trail," Renny rumbled softly.

"The rooming house is a labyrinth of a place," Doc continued. "There are at least three entrances and exits. That means each of you will have one to guard, while I go up and flush the game."

"Let's go," Long Tom said grimly.

One entrance to the rooming establishment—by stretching a little it might have been called a hotel—was through a gloomy drinking place which had sawdust and wooden sand box garboons on the floor. Another entrance was a blowsy door with a sign, "Beds 15c, 25c, 50c." The third gave into an alley and was probably as much used as any of the others. Doc stationed his men.

The bartender in the drinking place also ran the rooms, collecting for them at least. When Doc entered, he sidled over and spoke.

"Some of them fellers you was askin' about just left," he said.

Doc described Ben Brasken quickly.

"Was that one with them?" he asked.

"Nope. Not unless he went out one of the other doors. They do sometimes, you know. Don't make no difference to me. Everybody pays in advance here."

The proprietor seemed all right. He could not have any Chesterfield manners and run a place like this.

Doc mounted the stairs quickly. Ben Brasken was ensconced in a room which he had secured all for himself by paying for the three beds it contained. Or Ben Brasken's companions had paid for the room, rather.

Doc gained the door, listened outside it. He remained there for a long time. There was no sound of anything living within the room. Doc turned the knob. The door was unlocked. The bronze man went in.

Ben Brasken was there.

Doc backed out of the room and called his men. They gathered around the bronze man and looked at Ben Brasken. The looks they directed at Ben Brasken were short, and afterward they looked everywhere but at Ben Brasken.

"This makes it tough," Renny rumbled grimly, "unless Monk and Ham turned up something in New York."

Johnny drew a sheet over Ben Brasken to shut off the sight. For Ben Brasken's head had been practically cut off.

Chapter IX

THE STOLEN AIRSHIP

MONK and Ham, who had been left behind in New York City to do various things, were quarreling. This would have surprised no one who knew them. Rather, it would have been a surprise if they had not been squabbling.

"You'll let me examine that nickel," Ham was saying, "or I'll separate you from your epidermis!"

"That nickel," Monk grumbled, "was a perfectly ordinary nickel!"

This was a falsehood. The nickel had two heads. Monk had just used it to flimflam Ham into going out to get their morning ration of coffee and doughnuts.

"You mistake of nature!" Ham gritted. "We're going to match over again!"

"Any more argument out of you," Monk stated, "and I'll pop you so hard your spirit will have a heck of a time locating your body again!"

They were in Doc Savage's waterfront hangar, a large brick building on the Hudson River which masqueraded as a warehouse. A sign on the front said, "Hidalgo Trading Company." The building was actually a giant, almost bombproof, surrounded by burglar alarms, and held a number of planes, ranging from small single-seater true-gyros to huge transport ships. Moreover, there was a small and unusual submarine, some surface boats, including a diminutive but fast yacht.

The most interesting object, however, was probably the small demountable dirigible which Doc Savage had lately acquired, an all-metal craft which was not large, but which was the only one of its kind in existence.

It had only two motors, and one small cabin, enclosed within the gas bag. It had a high speed, and was small enough that it could be used to land men in a jungle, for instance, simply by tossing out a grappling hook which would snag a treetop. Moreover, it was stout enough that it could stand a good deal of banging around without damage.

Monk and Ham were watching this dirigible in particular. Kit Merrimore had wanted to buy it.

Monk picked up an envelope, took some papers out, and shuffled through them elaborately.

"I wonder if we'd better telegraph this stuff to Doc?" he pondered aloud. "He wanted information, whatever we could pick up, about a man named Martin Space."

Ham glared at Monk, tapping a toe indignantly.

"Are you gonna get that coffee and sinkers, you fashion plate shyster?" Monk demanded.

"Let me see that nickel!" Ham commanded.

"You'll see stars if you don't get going," Monk said.

A shrill buzzer whined out. It was connected with a button at the door.

Monk went to a device of mirrors by which they could view the vicinity of the door.

"Blazes!" he squeaked. "It's that girl, Kit Merrimore!"

Ham gasped, "She's been hurt!"

THE girl was draped against the door, hanging to the huge handle. She was pale. Her garments were torn. Her right sleeve from the shoulder down was soaked with red.

Monk gasped, "She may be dying!" and started for the door.

"Wait a minute, nickelwits!" Ham snapped.

"Huh?"

"This may be a trick. The hangar here is literally a fortress, and they may know it."

"Yeah," Monk paused. "I'll take a good look around."

He used a pair of binoculars on the wide, almost deserted water-front street. This was Sunday, and there was not much traffic.

"Nobody in sight," Monk decided.

"Be careful," Ham warned.

"Sure."

Monk was careful. He got a boat hook, opened the door a bare crack. The girl was now a limp heap on the grimy pavement outside.

Monk hooked the boat hook in the belt of her

sport frock, and gingerly hauled her inside without exposing himself.

Ham stood back in the meantime, his supermachine pistol held ready.

"Just like you to shoot a woman!" Monk sneered at him.

"These wouldn't damage her," Ham snapped. "They're mercy bullets. Only make her unconscious."

"She's that now," Monk told him.

Having closed the door and fastened it, the homely chemist growled, "We'd better rush her to a hospital," and bent over the young woman."

With his pocketknife, Monk opened the young woman's sleeve from wrist to shoulder.

He stared. His mouth fell open.

"Huh!" he exploded. "She's not hurt!"

A smacking sound caused him to glance around.

Ham had fallen face down.

Monk made a frantic effort to stand up, but instead, pitched down across Ham.

MONK, when he opened his eyes, and found himself looking at Ham, who seemed to be awake, made a disgusted face.

"Next time," Monk croaked gloomily, "I'll let you shoot her, and won't ask whether you've got mercy bullets or not."

"Next time," Ham snarled, "I'll have sense enough to pay no attention to you, you stumblebum, when I suspect there may be danger!"

They stopped abusing each other, and looked around. One thing struck them with the effects of a cold bath.

"The dirigible!" Monk howled.

"Gone!"

Their shouts were hardly necessary. There was not the slightest doubt but that the dirigible was gone. It must had been taken out through the big rolling doors at the river end of the hangar, because one of the doors had been improperly closed.

Four men were loitering about the hangar. Monk

and Ham had never seen any of the four previously, but they had seen crooks before.

The girl, Kit Merrimore, walked up to Monk and Ham, who had by now realized they were tied hand and foot with stout wire.

"Feel sick?" she asked.

"Yeah," Monk said. "Of embarrassment."

"That gas generally makes them sick at their stomachs," the girl said. "A nice old man I know who works for a chemical concern in New Jersey made it up for me. He said it would knock an elephant out almost instantly."

"Skip it," Monk requested.

"Oh, I like to brag," the young woman smiled. "I had the stuff in a bottle in my sport suit pocket, and I managed to pull the cork while you were ripping my sleeve to examine the wound that wasn't there. You certainly ruined my frock, incidentally."

Monk looked at her. In spite of himself, he grinned.

"How long we been out?" Monk asked.

"About six hours," the girl said.

Monk looked stunned. It hadn't seemed like more than a few minutes.

"We borrowed your dirigible," said the young woman.

They knew that already.

THE young woman now snapped her fingers, called out softly, and there was a stir over to the left. Two animals approached. Habeas Corpus, Monk's pet pig, which had thin, long legs and ears built for flying. And Ham's what-is-it, Chemistry.

Both animals frolicked around the young woman's trim ankles, a behavior which moved Monk and Ham to stare with unbelieving astonishment. Each man had spent innumerable hours training his pet, and a major item had been lessons in not to take up with strangers. Never before had it happened. Monk and Ham were mutually disgusted.

"Ham," Monk said, "for years, you've been wanting to have that hog for breakfast. You can have him. What's more, I'll help you eat him."

"Monk," Ham said as solemnly, "you can put Chemistry's hide over your fireplace, like you've been wanting to do."

The young woman smiled sweetly at them.

"In that case," she murmured, "I'll just take these two animals with me. I think they're real cute."

Monk and Ham groaned together.

One of the men came forward and growled. "We'd better blow, miss. No point in sticking around here any longer."

He pounced upon Monk and Ham and proceeded to make each one swallow a pill. The pills were about the size of Mexican beans, and each one was as bitter as anything either man had ever tasted.

Monk and Ham lay there grimacing, spitting out the bitter taste, and wondered what would happen. They soon found out. Things began to go away in a grayish haze.

The last thing they heard was the girl, Kit Merrimore, thanking them in sugary tones for Habeas Corpus and Chemistry.

Chapter X

SEA TRAIL

TWENTY hours later, Monk and Ham were back on their usual basis. Mutual sorrow over the shortcomings of their pets had caused them to be halfway civil to each other for a while, but that had not lasted very long.

"That goriboon of yours," Monk growled, coining a word, "was responsible for my Habeas taking up with that female hell-cat!"

"A soft touch for anything in skirts, you and your hog," Ham sneered.

"I think," Monk remarked, "that I'll see how you bounce."

They glared at each other. Monk was flying their plane with one hand, and had the other made into a fist, ready for knocking purposes.

The plane was over Nevada, just north of Reno, more exactly and was high. It would have been bitingly cold in the cabin, but they had the port closed and the heaters on. They were flying toward San Francisco.

Both Monk and Ham were a bit pale. The pills had not been poison, as they had both thought for a few horrible moments, but had merely rendered them generally useless for several hours. In truth, neither felt too spry yet, and it was reflected in the temper of their quarreling, which lacked its usual violence.

The radio loud-speaker—the silent cabin permitted use of the speaker instead of headsets—broke vociferously upon their diversion.

"KPOX to WDOC," the speaker said.

KPOX was the Denver police radio station, and WDOC was the plane.

"Yeah?" Monk said.

"The network of Western police stations have managed to gather only one more report of your dirigible," the police operator explained. "A filling station attendant on Highway 40 at a place called Vernal in Utah reported the coyotes' howling woke him up last night and he came out and saw a dirigible heading west. From what he said, I guessed it had come down to get

51

its bearings, then went up in the, the—whatcha call it?"

"Stratosphere," Monk supplied.

"Uh-huh. Plenty high. Anyway, there's no more reports."

"Thanks a lot."

Monk clicked off the mike and looked at Ham.

Ham said, "The dirigible was sighted in Pennsylvania, then at a place called Millard, in Missouri. And now this. They headed west. But a fat chance we have of finding them."

Monk nodded gloomily.

By the time they met Doc Savage in San Francisco, Monk and Ham were not on speaking terms. Each looked slightly bruised, and their clothing had a few tears. It was to be suspected they had come to blows. It was a strange feud they carried on, considering that each would lay down his life for the other.

Doc was not in a cheerful frame of mind.

It was impossible to tell this by looking at the bronze man. He never showed emotion. But Renny, Long Tom and Johnny looked as if they were sitting around in a dead friend's parlor.

Monk, uneasy because he and Ham had let the dirigible be stolen from them, tried to cover it up by a big grin.

"You guys look as if you had been seeing ghosts," he said.

"We have," Renny said.

"Huh?" Monk grunted, startled by the soberness with which Renny had spoken.

"We're up against something we can't understand," Renny rumbled quietly.

"You mean you've found no trace of that Lupp, Two-bit and the girl, Kit Merrimore?" Monk asked.

"No," Renny said, "They have disappeared, and although we've had the police and private detective agencies looking for them, and doing all we could ourselves, we have had no luck. Poor Ben Brasken was buried this morning. They murdered him to keep him from talking."

Renny took in a deep sigh. Long Tom swallowed.

Johnny fiddled absentmindedly with his monocle. There was something strange about all their attitudes.

"Look here!" Monk said suddenly. "What's eating you birds?"

Renny looked at Doc. "You tell him, Doc."

The bronze man seemed to consider for a time.

"You know about the city of Ost which Ben Brasken claimed he visited, and which the sailors on the *Benny Boston* are sure they saw?" Doc asked.

"Sure," Monk grunted. "What about it? Obviously, there ain't no such city."

"Let us have a little demonstration," Doc said.

The bronze man went to the bureau in the hotel room, picked up the strange flatiron-shaped piece of metal which he had found in the cubby in the bow of the *Benny Boston,* and handed it to Monk.

"Blazes!" Monk exploded. "What am I supposed to do with this?"·

"Just hold it," Doc replied.

"Say, what kind of a gag is this?"

Big-fisted Renny put in, "Try to do something that may, for you, be kinda hard, Monk. Just keep your mouth shut and stand there for a few minutes."

Monk, looking skeptical and half convinced that some kind of trick was in the making, held the piece of iron in his hands. It was the first time he had seen it, so he turned it slowly, examining it.

But as Monk continued to hold the iron block, a change came over his features. He blinked his eyes three or four times. He looked down at the block.

An absolute and stark amazement came over Monk's face.

"For the love of Mike!" he gasped.

He dropped the block and sprang away from it.

HAM let out one cracking guffaw, then sobered. "What's the matter, you missing link?" he demanded. Monk said nothing. That was unusual for Monk.

Doc Savage said quietly, "Ham, you might find it interesting to try what Monk just tried."

Ham looked confused, and gulped, "You—think so?" rather inanely.

When no one spoke, Ham moved over and gingerly picked up the block. Where he had been sarcastic and skeptical a moment ago, he was now doubtful and confused.

He held the block. Nothing appeared to happen, and this caused a sardonic grin to creep on his lips. Then the grin straightened out slowly and vanished, then his lips parted slightly, and incredulity dilated his eyes.

He put the block down as if it were hot.

"Wise guy," Monk said. "Now what do you say?"

"Describe your sensation as you held that block, Ham," Doc Savage suggested.

Instead of doing so, Ham suddenly yelled, "What caused that?"

"Suppose you first describe what you felt," Doc persisted.

Ham whipped out a handkerchief and blotted his forehead.

"It was a *feeling,* all right," he said slowly. "And that is what floors me. As I stood there with that iron block in my hands, I naturally thought about what we know of its history. And suddenly I had the feeling that Ost was real, and furthermore, I got a sensation of another sort—kind of—"

"As if a guy were pointing a gun at you." Monk supplied.

"Yes." Ham agreed. "Only not a feeling of any definite weapon menacing me. Just a feeling of something—something horrible—about to happen."

MONK and Ham stood there registering emotions of two fellows who had just met up with something they could not comprehend.

Monk got his startled thoughts back on solid ground. He snorted loudly to show that he was not buffaloed.

"I'm gonna put that iron block under an X ray," he said.

"We already did that," Doc Savage told him. "The block is solid iron."

Monk, nonplused for a moment, thought of something else.

"Then I'll try some chemical tests on it," he declared.

Doc Savage said, "We have given the iron block a chemical analysis. It is an ordinary iron block. No chemicals, no other elements that those which go into ordinary iron."

Monk scratched his nubbin of a head, then pulled one of his ears which bore traces of past fights. "Then how do you explain that feeling?"

The homely chemist looked at Doc Savage as he asked for an accounting of the phenomenon. A natural act. Monk had an enormous respect for the bronze man's abilities.

Doc would have an idea of what was behind the mystery if anybody would have one.

In his heart, Monk did not expect Doc to answer his question. He was astonished when Doc spoke.

"On the face of the thing, it is impossible," Doc Savage said quietly.

Monk blinked. "You mean its got you buffaloed?"

"Something like that."

"Blazes!" Monk muttered. "Blazes!"

IT was the first time in Monk's recollection that the bronze man had admitted being confronted with a mystery to which he could see no possible explanation. One had to know Doc to appreciate what that really meant.

"There is a simple explanation somewhere," Doc Savage added, "because every one knows there is an explanation for everything that happens."

"Yeah," Monk scratched his head again. "But what are we gonna do about this?"

"The *Benny Boston* is sailing to-night on her regular run to Melbourne," Doc Savage replied. "We are going to be aboard her.

"The *Benny Boston* is a clue of sorts. You will recall that the city of Ost was seen from the old steamer on more than one voyage. Therefore, we will sail aboard her, in hopes of seeing Ost. If we do, we may be able to make something out of the phenomenon."

"Phenomenon?"

Doc seemed not to hear the question, which made Monk look very thoughtful, because on past occasions the bronze man had acted in that manner when he had a suspicion which was no more than that, and which he did not wish to discuss.

They went aboard the *Benny Boston* secretly, letting no one know who they were.

Chapter XI

THE WATCHFUL WAIT

FIFTY years or so ago, almost every ship that sailed the seas carried a few passengers. Nowadays, it is different. But the *Benny Boston* had been built fifty years ago, maybe more, and she had never been materially changed. She had a few cabins for passengers. They were not much.

The plumbing was china pitchers and washbowls, and you threw the water out the porthole after you had washed your hands. The berths were really berths, with a high board in front so you didn't roll out. The board was necessary, too, because the *Benny Boston* in a seaway had a way of rolling like a hog in a mud puddle with lice along its backbone.

Ham, who liked the élite comforts of ultramodern civilization, lifted his upper lip up against his finely chiseled nose when he looked over the accommodations.

"Putrid," he said.

Doc and his aids had boarded the *Benny Boston* in the night, and no one knew their identity, not even Captain Smooth, the skipper.

There was a bustle on the pier and below decks, because some late cargo had apparently arrived, and had to be loaded aboard before sailing time.

"Going to look things over," Doc Savage said, and left his associates in their connecting cabins.

The bronze man wore dark clothing, including a long, dark raincoat, and although he usually wore no hat, he wore one now, a large one with a wide brim which he bent down all around and shadowed his features.

He prowled the decks, not in a rambling fashion, but in a way that showed he was interested in one thing more than anything else.

Doc worked forward. The late-arrived freight was being loaded into the hatch just aft of the bow. That meant it was large freight. Small stuff they would have trundled up a sloping runway into a door in the side of the hull.

The bronze man found a secluded spot on the forward rail, in the obscurity beside an elevator, and watched. The boxes were new, large, not all the same size.

Box after box came aboard. Doc watched closely. The boxes were new. There was an electric light beside the hatch, and when the boxes swung past it, he could read the name of the consignee:

AUSTRALIAN FARM MACHINERY CO.
MELBOURNE, AUSTRALIA

Doc watched for fully fifteen minutes.

Then a strange thing happened: There came into existence a tiny, trilling sound, small, fantastic, almost impossible for any one who overheard it to describe. A tremulous note, it ran up and down the musical scale, not a whistle, and yet not a product of vocal cords, either.

This was the small sound which the bronze man made unconsciously on occasion when he was profoundly moved with surprise, or in moments of mental stress.

There was a very good reason for it now: He had made a discovery.

DOC SAVAGE left his niche beside the elevator, worked aft, descended a companionway, moved a few paces, went down another companionway, and was soon in the hold where they were stowing the late-arrived freight.

He did not go near the stevedores, and did not let them see him. Seemingly in no hurry, he waited. After a time, the last box came in. The stevedores departed finally and silence fell.

Doc waited. Sometimes, a tool or something was forgotten, and a man returned for it. When enough time had elapsed that no danger remained of this happening, he went to one of the boxes.

Their shape and size had interested him.

Furthermore, the *Benny Boston* happened to be the only steamer sailing for Australia immediately. The next one would not depart for ten days, to be exact.

The pine boards which composed one box had a flaw in one spot. A small finger grip was afforded. Doc took hold and performed a rather remarkable feat of strength in tugging off the board.

He reached into the box and felt around.

His small, trilling sound came out briefly. It was tiny, hardly louder than the drone of some small insect on the wing.

He put a flashlight beam into the box.

The box held the starboard stern collapsible gas-bag section of Doc's little dirigible.

He replaced the board. Working quickly, he gained entrance to two of the other boxes. There was no doubt of it by the time he had finished. The thieves had selected the *Benny Boston* for shipping the dirigible.

The dirigible, then, had been seized for a flight in the South Seas, or some equally distant part. Why the aircraft had not been flown there was a question simply answered.

It is a long distance across the Pacific Ocean. And the dirigible, without special engine fuel of which Doc Savage probably had the only supply available, was not capable, for instance, of even making the San Francisco-Honolulu jump safely. With the special fuel, it could make an infinitely greater hop. But the thieves would not have that.

Having learned all that was necessary—the name of shipper and cosignee on the boxes were undoubtedly fakes—Doc turned away. He walked toward the companionway.

The round, iron hardness of a gun against his face stopped him.

"You've stepped into plenty of trouble!" a harsh voice rumbled.

Doc maintained a wise stillness. Ebony was not blacker than the darkness around him. He wore a watch, but it was a special silent kind, and only a keen ear, placed against the case, could detect its ticking.

Yet it seemed audible in the stillness. The one with the gun was holding his breath. He let it out with a careful slowness.

"Renny," Doc said.

"Holy cow!" Renny thumped softly.

"Our airship is in these boxes."

"Yeah, that's what I suspected," Renny agreed. "I sneaked out on deck, watched the loading, and it suddenly dawned on me that the boxes were about the right size. I waited until everything had quieted down, then came below for a look. Nobody saw me.

"I saw your light poking into the boxes, but couldn't make out that it was you. I thought it was one of the gang making sure the shipment was intact."

"It is all there, apparently," Doc said. "We had better get back to our stateroom."

Both made the return without attracting attention. Most of the crew had probably gone ashore for a final fling.

Monk and the others opened their mouths when they heard about the dirigible being aboard.

Dapper Ham, who had been putting a fresh coating of unconsciousness-producing chemical on his sword cane tip, had a happy deduction.

"If the airship is aboard, the gang is probably on the boat, too," he said.

"A possibility," Doc agreed.

Monk, looking very cheerful, rubbed his hands together.

"This is a break for us," he growled. "Maybe I'll get a chance to get my hog back."

Ham snorted. "From the way he took up with that crowd, my guess is that your hog won't have anything to do with you. Good riddance."

"That what-is-it of yours made up to the girl first!" Monk gritted.

"That's a lie, you lump of gristle and hair!" Ham replied.

Renny interruped with a rumble.

"That quarrel is gonna have to recess," he declared. "We're not attracting any attention in here. Another squawk out of either of you, and I'll take you both!"

"Any time you're feeling lucky!" Monk and Ham said in chorus.

Chapter XII

ADRIFT

THREE weeks. Twenty-one days. Five hundred and four hours. Thirty thousand two hundred and forty-minutes. A long time.

After that much time had passed, Monk and Ham were getting along fairly well, strangely enough. Or possibly it was not so strange, for Renny was about to eat them both, as he put it earnestly. Renny had appointed himself silencer in the matter of arguments, and was doing a good job.

Renny did not often put his foot down so vehemently. Moreover, when he sat in a corner and cracked walnuts in his huge fists, it was convincing, somehow. They were not English walnuts, but the black ones, the thick-hulled kind.

Monotony had done about as much damage to their nerves as it could do. Nothing had happened in the three weeks, except that the ancient hooker *Benny Boston* had cut more didoes in a seaway than a washtub in the Niagara rapids. They took their exercises in the stateroom, and had their meals there.

They told their steward they were seasick. That was the truth part of the time, as far as Monk, Johnny and Long Tom were concerned. The steward had never seen all of them.

There was a reason for their keeping under cover. Long Tom, taking a constitutional the first night out, when every one but the watch on duty had turned in, had come upon an old newspaper in the bedraggled lounge. In it was an article about Doc Savage and pictures of the bronze man and his five aids.

That meant Doc and his party would be recognized as soon as they did any extensive promenading. So they had kept in.

Each day, Doc Savage spent two hours in exercise, sometimes a bit more. He used a routine, varying a little each day, which he had been engaged in using since childhood.

Through the porthole, the group had been able to

observe some of the other passengers, although not many. The *Benny Boston* had had rough going, and only the hardy souls were on deck.

There were a number of passengers. This was in itself suspicious, because the *Benny Boston* was no liner. All the passengers, however, were hardly enemies, from their appearance. There were even women, some of them young.

On the night of the twenty-first day out, Monk kicked over the traces. It was only a question of time until he was bound to do this, anyway.

Monk was not by nature a watchful, waiting soul. He did not entirely approve of Doc Savage's intention of waiting until they were near Melbourne, Australia, their first stop, before instituting a sudden searching of the ship and unmasking of the villains, if any.

Doc was waiting until they were near Melbourne because it would be a shorter run to port with the prisoners, with a correspondingly smaller time for them to try to escape.

The *Benny Boston* was nowhere near Australia as yet. She was somewhere off the coast of New Guinea. The wilder part of that coast, too.

When Monk kicked over the traces, he left the cabin while the others were sleeping, and strolled down the deck getting a breath of sea air. Their cabins rather smelled, as cabins on old boats will. The *Benny Boston* had given the impression of carrying skunks in her bilge.

Monk had not strolled far when he saw a woman leaning against the rail. She was alone. She looked slender, and therefore she was probably young.

A woman was the downfall of Sampson, and as far as Monk was concerned, history repeated itself.

He went over and struck up a conversation.

"KIND of a rough trip, huh?" he asked, propping an elbow on the rail a discreet distance from the young lady.

Monk was an old hand at this stuff. Somewhat

strange, that, since his looks frequently scared fierce bulldogs back under their porches.

"Eet ees bad," the young woman said.

"You bet," Monk agreed. "Now I know why they make portholes small."

"Why, *m'sieu'?*"

"If mine had been larger, I would have got out and swam," Monk replied.

This got the chuckle he had hoped for. She had a nice voice. She was probably a looker. These French babies were generally pretty snappy.

"I guess the ship is off New Guinea," Monk said. "Probably not more than sixty miles or so. That storm drove us a little out of our course."

Monk knew this because Doc had taken some observations through a porthole.

"*Qui,*" the young lady agreed. "Ze captain ees tell me zat."

So she knew the captain. It was a cinch she was a good looker then. Captains always picked off the peaches.

"I bet your husband is seasick," Monk suggested.

She laughed again. Very nice.

"Zey always ask zat," she chuckled. "*Non.* I 'ave no oosban'."

"Swell," Monk said. "You like Australia?"

"*Oui!*" the young woman replied quickly. "I love ze seety of Melbourne."

"Live there?"

"*Oui.*"

Great stuff, Monk thought. Get her telephone number, then persuade Doc to hang around Melbourne for a while.

Monk opened his mouth to tell her she should see his pet pig, then remembered he didn't have any. A tough break, that one. Habeas Corpus had a way with the girls, Monk had discovered. Monk could lead Habeas down Fifth or Park Avenues any day and make half a dozen conquests.

Before Monk could think up another subject for conversation, the young woman turned from the rail.

"Au revoir," she murmured sweetly. "I theenk I will retire now."

"Nuts!" Monk thought, but he said, "Pleasant sleep, and I'll see you again sometime."

That was the stuff. Don't let them think you were chasing them.

The young woman walked away, and the night took her. Monk had not seen her face, but there was no doubt in his mind but that she would do. For that matter, if she had taken a look at him, he had not observed it.

Oh, well, she'd see him in the daytime, and his was the kind of hairy beauty that seemed to impress the femmes.

Monk went below in a happy frame of mind and turned in.

He got a lucky break, then. He could not get the young woman off his mind, and he had done nothing for days but sleep and quarrel with Ham when Renny was not watching, so he was not sleepy anyway.

He laid awake with his thoughts.

That was how he happened to see the puddle of stuff come creeping under the door.

Monk liked to sleep with all his pillows and sometimes a suitcase under his head. Ham claimed this was because his close ancestors had roosted upright in the trees with the monkeys and birds.

Monk saw the stuff coming under the door immediately. He thought it was water, and reflected that it was not raining, and he had not heard a sea break on deck which would send water into the corridor.

Then he got a whiff. Monk was a chemist. He knew what things were when he smelled them.

And he retained his presence of mind. Springing out of bed, he made no sound. Nor did he make a noise in scooping up the bedclothes, carrying them over and depositing them on top of the puddle spreading from under the door.

Monk held his breath.

He ran into the connecting cabins which the others

occupied. He looked at the doors. Other puddles were spreading there.

He awakened the men quickly.

"Poison gas!" he breathed. "Quiet!"

The activity for the next few moments was wild but silent. It was Doc Savage who seized the rest of the bedclothing and spread it over the liquid, which had obviously been poured under the doors from the corridor. Then he opened the windows.

It was the bronze man, too, who really saved them. He did it by hurriedly opening his equipment cases which held chemicals, getting out various bottles, mixing the contents quickly in one of the big washbowls, and pouring the concoction over the saturated bedclothing.

A yellowish vapor arose, but this was harmless. The chemicals Doc had added to the gas liquid had rendered it harmless, just as water added to alcohol in quantities makes it noninflammable.

"Whoever poured the stuff under the doors probably fled immediately," Doc said. "They won't be back, but will wait for our bodies to be found."

Renny growled, "What I want to know is, how did they discover us?"

Monk had been doing some tall wondering on that point. And Monk, while he was a fellow who lacked discretion at times, firmly believed that confession is good for the soul.

"I don't think I done it," he said.

"You ape!" Ham grated instantly. "What have you been up to?"

"Aw, I hadda have some air," Monk explained. "I went on deck."

Ham sighed. "Well, if nobody saw you, that don't explain it."

"No, it couldn't have been me," Monk agreed. "The girl wasn't one of the gang."

Ham almost yelled at that. "What girl?"

"A French oo-la-la," Monk elaborated. "But she was just a passenger, and lived in Melbourne."

"Was she about the size of Kit Merrimore?" Doc Savage asked abruptly.

"Well, now——" Monk floundered. As a matter of fact, the girl had been about the size of Kit Merrimore.

"I examined Kit Merrimore's past," Doc Savage stated. "She was at one time an actress, and her best part was that of a French girl in America."

Monk emitted a feeble squeak.

"Catch me, somebody," he croaked. "I think I'm going to faint."

Ham said grimly, "Renny!"

"Huh?"

"How about letting me cut him up in little pieces?" Ham demanded.

"Go ahead," Renny directed.

"And I'll stand still for you," Monk contributed, after which they did not have the heart to roast him to the brownness that they would have liked.

It was now apparent that the enemy was not only aboard, but was going to make trouble. Doc's group hurriedly set about opening their equipment cases which held such weapons as they thought they might need.

They had hardly started on this task when a face appeared at the porthole. It was a face Doc's men knew. The owner was one of the men who had been with Kit Merrimore at the dirigible stealing in New York.

The face disappeared instantly.

Doc flung to the porthole. It was open. He thrust his head through. The man was legging it down the deck.

Several men were gathered toward the bow. Doc looked in the direction of the stern. More men gathered there.

There was a cheap leather suitcase standing under the porthole, on deck.

Doc whipped back out of the porthole.

"Run!" he said, and his voice was a crash.

Doc's men had learned to do things quickly when the bronze man spoke like that, and they dived through the doors into the corridor, and when Doc gestured, dashed down the corridor.

Something hit the ship as if it were a great drum. The doors fell into the corridor. The old carpet jumped up off the floor. The light bulbs broke and came jingling down; only no one heard them jingle, because sound had pushed eardrums in and strained them until they could hear nothing for moments.

Probably Doc Savage was the only one who knew what had happened. His friends had not seen the suitcase. Had they, they were astute enough to guess it held explosive.

The bronze man was bringing out small objects and hurling them first one direction in the corridor, then another. They were smoke bombs, and blackness bloated up and engulfed the group, and it was darker than it had ever seemed to be before.

A gun banged, and another, and a small machine gun snarled like an iron bulldog. Bullets pecked and sizzled.

"Top deck," Doc Savage said. "Get together with me."

His associates got together with him.

"Your supermachine pistol, Renny," Doc said. "Demolition cartridges. The ceiling."

"Holy cow!" Renny said, which was the equivalent of O. K., and they stood there a minute.

Renny's supermachine pistol hooted; explosive-driven air buffeted them, and wood and metal fell. The *Benny Boston's* rusted old whistle started on a long toot, while all over the hooker men yelled, cursed and shot off their guns.

There was a hole in the ceiling now. Renny had made it with his little supermachine pistol bullets that were packed with high-powered hell. It was a big hole, and parts of the ceiling hung down, so that by grabbing and hauling, Doc and his men climbed out.

The smoke bomb smoke poured out around them. They got out of the smoke. The stars looking down at them seemed small, the moon big, a little red as if blushing.

Doc and his men started for the bridge, but red sparks sprang up along the bridge rail, and bullets began making those strange, awful sounds which nothing, but bullets make.

"Gas!" Monk squeaked. "We've got some!"

"They have gas masks, too." Doc pointed out.

Men ran here and there, mostly fore and aft, and once in a while they were in a spot where there was some light, and it could be seen that they were wearing gas masks and iron military hats.

"The ventilation funnels to the engine room," Doc said. "If we control the engine room, we control the ship."

Ventilators, flower-mouthed monsters, reared up from the top deck all around. Doc ran to one of these, sprang, caught the lip. Hanging half inside, he listened. It would be easy to go down, bracing his back and hands against one side, his feet against the other. But he did not go down. He listened.

Then he slapped his hands against the ventilator, making sounds.

A big, nonexistent snake hissed in the bottom. Hot steam came up. Scalding clouds of it. Men had been waiting with steam hoses at the bottom, and they had thought Doc was coming down.

A searchlight came on, splashed Doc's little group. Monk shot it out. Bullets traveled about without much system. But fore and aft, the attackers were organizing themselves for a charge.

Captain Smooth had had his ship taken away from him by now.

"The boats," Doc Savage said.

LONG TOM exploded, "You mean we're going to get off the ship?"

"Right."

"But we may be able to lick them!"

"Maybe. But we are leaving the ship anyway."

"Why?"

"A good reason," the bronze man said. "Quick! The third boat on the starboard is a motor dory."

There was no inclination for a lengthy debate on whys. Doc's group got the boat down to the water. The boat was the one modern thing about the *Benny Bos-*

ton, or rather, the davits by which it was lowered were. They were the type which could be operated mechanically from the boat.

Doc and his men got into the boat. Two of the group watched the controls. The others used flashlights and machine pistols. The flashlights gave bright light. The machine pistols gave out streams of mercy bullets at the right time.

The boat was now adrift. The *Benny Boston* went gurgling past, and the boat rocked and turned completely around twice in the boil pushed back by the propellers.

The dory had shipped a little water. Monk and Ham bailed. Doc did things with the motor and it began making noises; the bow of the lifeboat picked up, the stern settled down, and they made ten knots or so.

"Diesel," Doc Savage said of the motor. "It will run a long time on what fuel we have."

The bronze man and his aids were not as worried as landlubbers might have been. The *Benny Boston* had put about, it was true, and it could run them down as easily as a drunken motorist would run down a pup, if it found them.

If it found them. This was the open sea. There had been storms for days. It was calm now. But big swells kicked up by the storms were still rolling mountain high, and it was dark.

The only searchlight on the *Benny Boston* had been shot out. As long as the ship showed no light, Doc's little band was in no great danger of being picked up. And they would not show a light.

Twenty minutes put them in safety.

And Long Tom got around to finding out why they had left the ship in the open sea, when there still remained a chance that they could have overcome their foes. A very good chance, from what Long Tom knew of Doc Savage.

"I don't see yet," the electrical wizard said, "why we gave up the ship."

Doc pointed. "There is the reason."

They all looked, and they all saw.

"Ost!" Monk breathed.

Monk was awed—It was rarely that he was awed.

Ost! The little band had heard about it. Now they were seeing it. Fantastic vision of the sea. All had read its description as printed in the newspapers. It was all of that.

Ost was high. It was as if it sat upon a distant mountainside, yet they could not see a mountain, and they could see the city.

Luminous. Like a photograph done, by some unknown process, in the radioactive stuff which is put on watches and clocks to make them tell time in the dark. And like that radioactive material when seen from a distance, this picture was indistinct. It seemed to be a trifle out of focus.

A city, it had been called. It was more of a town. There were buildings, dwellings or places where businesses were conducted, if this weird place had businesses.

Pyramids, these buildings. Every one of them. Broad at the bottom, sloping up, somewhat erratically, as if there was a porch or veranda every so often.

Topping each pyramid was an irregular something, tall, narrow. It was impossible to distinguish, due to the indistinctness of the image, what these topping things were.

Strangest of all, though, was the building at the back of the city. The big structure. A pyramid, too, but it was upside down. Inverted. Suspended in the air, apparently.

Hanging upside down with nothing to hold it.

Monk laughed. Did it suddenly, loudly, somewhat irrationally.

And somehow no one was surprised at the laugh, or even looked around. It was the perfectly natural thing to do. The thing they were viewing was too impossible, of course.

"Well, now we've got to figure out what we're seeing," Ham said.

"If it's a slide thrown from a powerful magic lantern on the *Benny Boston,* we should be able to see the light of the lantern," Long Tom contributed. "The *Benny Boston* is behind us."

But the group could see no magic-lantern glow.

Gaunt Johnny picked from a pocket a pair of binoculars which he had been carrying there. He studied the vision with the binoculars.

"I'll be superamalgamated!" he exploded.

"Eh?" Monk demanded.

"Look," Johnny said, and handed the homely chemist the glasses.

Monk looked. He put the glasses down, and said something that was only a mumble of astonishment.

"What's the matter with you two silly-sallies?" Ham asked sarcastically.

"Nothing," Johnny muttered.

"Yeah," Monk said. "Nothing except that these binoculars don't magnify that city."

"Don't magnify it? The glasses do not——"

"See for yourself," Monk invited.

Ham looked, and when he put the glasses down, his manner showed that they hadn't done their duty.

"Somebody took the lenses out as a joke!" he barked, an instant later.

But the lenses were in the glasses, and they magnified everything except what it was wanted most that they magnify now.

THERE was silence in the boat. Silence and eyestrain. Wonder. Bafflement.

"What's over there, Doc?" Monk asked at last.

"New Guinea," the bronze man said.

"How far?"

"Sixty miles or so."

"Nobody can see sixty miles at sea at night."

Doc Savage said nothing. No one else said anything. Doc headed the motorized lifeboat for the city.

No one talked much. They all watched what they could see high above the sea ahead. It was so wonderful, so amazing, that they did nothing but wonder and puzzle about it.

The little band hardly noticed the breeze when it kicked up. It was the type of breeze that always kicked up before dawn, and it turned into one of the vicious little squalls noted frequently happening in that part of the sea. Before long spray, and occasionally green water, was coming over the side of the boat.

Two thousand years ago, before the birth of Christ, the Norsemen built boats, open cockleshells fastened with thongs and wooden pins, and in them crossed the Atlantic. This lifeboat had lines like them, and it was perhaps not much smaller.

Doc and his men came through without much more hardship than a thorough wetting.

But the city was lost somewhere in the excitement and darkness and whining wind and stinging spray. They had been surprised at how long it had remained visible. Only near the height of the squall could they no longer see it; and after the squall had abated, they were too tired from their battle with the elements to show much interest in it. They lay down and slept as only exhausted men can.

Doc Savage remained awake and steered and nursed the fuel supply of the Diesel.

Between the big bronze man's feet as he stood at the tiller was an equipment case of metal. One of his own.

He had gotten it aboard during the excitement and none of the others had noticed.

Chapter XIII

THE SUMMONING VISION

Doc's men were glad to see the dawn—and they weren't. The sun was warm. Furthermore, it showed them land.

But it did not show them the city. There was no city. Johnny used his binoculars, and they magnified the land, so there was nothing wrong with the glasses.

The little band reached the land before noon. There was no city on it.

The shore was rocky, but here and there was a patch of dark, smooth sand, and they landed on one of these, hauled the lifeboat up, and tied the painter to a palm. There was fresh water and canned foods in the boat. The canned foods were good.

Captain Smooth, a hard man, had been a good seaman, and kept his lifeboat larders stocked. That was a good idea on a ship like the *Benny Boston,* when the boats might be needed at any time.

Doc and his men ate.

"I feel better," Monk said. He looked at the mountains, searching for the city, and not finding it, said grimly, "*Maybe* I feel better!"

"That's funny," Renny said. "I feel that way, too."

"If you mean, you have a sort of fear, I have it, also," said Long Tom.

Ham made a clucking noise. "I thought I was the only one who was scared. If you ask me, it's darned queer. There's nothing here to be scared of."

All stood there, looking, as Monk expressed it, funny. That is, they wore the expressions of men who could feel fear.

Then something happened which startled them all: Doc Savage's tiny fantastic, trilling sound came into being, rose and fell, and ebbed away into nothingness.

Doc's aids stared at the bronze man. The trilling never came without reason. Always it marked something of major importance. They waited for him to explain.

Doc did not explain.

"We are heading inland, he said.

"What for?" asked Monk, who was always full of questions.

Doc seemed not to hear. After that, there were no more inquiries. The bronze man, all knew, did not feel ready to explain.

The bronze man and his men took the food and water, and marched inshore. They were not too badly equipped. They would miss hammocks and mosquito netting, and perhaps antidotes for snake bites, although Doc might have that in the remarkable carry-all vest which he wore.

Doc Savage carried the metal equipment case which he had brought. It was the smallest of their assortment of cases. It seemed very heavy, even for Doc.

Once, Monk volunteered, "I'll carry that for a while, Doc," and picked the case up. The homely chemist immediately looked queer, and put the case down.

It was so heavy he could hardly lift it, much less carry it any distance.

There were palm trees around the party for a while. Then they began to climb, and there were no more palm trees. Palms grow best around salt water.

NIGHT saw all—with the exception of Doc—hot, tired and more or less quilled with thorns. They had made, at a liberal estimate, ten miles. It was not bad. It was, in fact, good, and they were proud of it, for the way had turned into one of the thickest jungles they had ever seen—when it was not straight up.

There was not much talk as the group cooked and made smudges to keep away the insects. There was a reason: The fear. It was still with them, and still they could not explain, identify or even fully comprehend it. Renny gave the best description of how it felt.

"The first time I sat in a front-line trench, knowing we were to go over the top, and not knowing the exact zero hour, I felt this same way," he said. "I guess I was scared. Don't know how else you would describe the feeling, although some lunkhead captain kept telling us good soldiers never got scared."

"Only mental defectives do not get scared," Doc Savage said. "Fear is a normal emotion. If you do not feel it, you are not normal."

"Then I'm too dang normal!" Renny grunted. "Right now, I don't feel a bit brave."

"Bravery is the power of determination that pushes you toward a goal when the natural instincts of fear urge you to turn back."

Doc and his men were now on their backs on pallets of soft boughs which they had plucked. The smudge fires were to windward, and the dense smoke lifted just enough to make a cover a few inches above their faces as the breeze carried it past.

"What I want to know," Monk complained, "is what is scaring us. Me, I ain't used to getting scared when there ain't nothing to get scared of."

All were too tired to stay awake long. They slept silently and deeply, except for long Johnny, who occasionally emitted a snore that disturbed the birds roosting in the surrounding jungle.

Doc Savage awakened his men once that night, and let them look at the city of Ost, which had become visible through the jungle. The vision was not much more distinct than it had been the night before, although perhaps a little.

When the sun came up, there was no city.

Doc Savage led the march onward. He carried the heavy metal equipment case, and seemed not to mind greatly its enormous weight, although the going was intensely difficult, almost impossible at times.

On such occasions as this, the real power of the enormous muscular development the bronze man had built up through years of exercise and living as strict, always, as an athlete in training, became a thing that amazed his aids.

Time after time, while they rested, gasping and perspiring, he would range through the jungle and come back with fruits and roots which, when eaten, had special strength-giving values.

The going became worse as the group progressed, a circumstance that seemed impossible.

They pushed ahead for nine days.

NINE days was a long time to march through green hell with nothing, actually, to urge them on. To be sure, Doc's band saw the fantastic city ahead frequently, but it was always like a mirage; and they realized it was much more distinct, yet it did not seem a lot closer.

They were a bedraggled crowd by now. There was only one whole shirt among them. Pants had been docked off above the knees, with the exception of Ham, who was still trying to preserve his sartorial splendor. Ham had the one whole shirt.

The night of the tenth day was an unsettled one. The five aids were convinced they were on a wild-goose chase, and when they thought of the terrible trek back to the coast, they felt like eating nails.

Doc Savage alone was an exception. He had not said what he felt. But he had not let down any in the forward drive.

Then Monk awoke in the night and saw the old man with the spider arms.

This strange apparition of a being stood on the far edge of the clearing in which they had camped for the night. There was bright moonlight. Yet moonlight at the best is not the finest illumination when it comes to showing up details. That made it stranger that Monk could see the fellow so well.

The being's face was wrinkled. Like a melon in a loose blue sack. Blue. His skin was distinctly blue. His garment seemed to be made out of one piece of dark-red cloth—simply a long piece of goods which he had wrapped this way and that around his body until he had it all covered. He had incredibly long arms which were very thin, and his legs were almost as thin, but only about a forth as long.

"Wake up, guys!" Monk barked. "Here's Goa!"

Monk was not as amazed then about what he had said as he was later.

The others awakened. They looked. All of them exclaimed in surprise.

And all five dashed forward. Doc Savage alone remained where he was.

The spider-armed old creature looked very happy when he saw them coming. He beckoned wildly, urging them to come on. Then he turned and ran on ahead of them.

The group shouted at him to stop, but he paid no attention. At intervals, he would wave at them to come on.

Doc's men did not gain on him. This surprised them, for they were running their fastest. Their quarry did not have legs built for running, if appearances were any indication.

But they were not half as surprised, though, as they were an instant later.

They came to a meadow of soft, deep grass. Monk glanced back. They were crushing down the grass with their feet, and leaving a plain trail.

But the old man ahead was leaving no tracks whatever.

"Hey!" Monk squawled. "There's somethin' phony!"

The others stopped. The bony, old man went on, still beckoning, and was lost in the dark jungle.

Monk and the others produced flashlights. They looked around, examining everything soft enough to have taken a footprint. They did not find a single track.

They went back to camp walking in the manner of small boys passing a cemetery after having heard a good ghost story. They told Doc Savage about it. The bronze man did not say what they expected.

"Anxious to go on now?" he queried.

"Darned right," Renny rumbled. "Holy cow! There's something blamed queer behind this, and I wanta get at the bottom of it."

There was more than a third of the night remaining. They had a little difficulty going to sleep.

"Monk," Ham said.

"What is it, you spook-chasing shyster?"

"When you awakened us, you said, 'Here's Goa.' What I'd like to know is, how you knew it was Goa. Did he call out his name while we were asleep?"

Monk made a startled, choking noise.

"Well, did he?"

Monk said, "I refuse to speak."

Ham chuckled. "If it'll make you feel any better, I knew his name was Goa, too. I don't know how I knew it. I just did."

All did sleep a little before dawn.

THIS jungle country was inhabited. Doc's group had seen signs of natives, footprints usually. A few times, they had seen furtive faces, but the natives had fled, and they had not bothered to try to make contact with them. Meeting a peaceful native tribe usually meant lengthy ceremonials, and they were in a hurry.

Doc Savage always led the way, flake gold eyes alert. Just how little his trained scrutiny missed was brought home to the others when, a little before noon, he stopped abruptly while striding along with seeming casualness.

"Back," he said.

He advanced a few paces alone, bent forward and scrutinized something. He went back to the others at once. "Poisoned thorns," Doc said. "We will have to take to the trees."

Ham demanded, "Can we not go around?"

"Easily. But we might not see the next ones. Natives are sometimes clever at handling them."

"Oh! You mean——"

"Yes," the bronze man replied. "They were thorns set by natives to trap other natives. We are now in war-like country."

Gaunt Johnny, the archaeologist, put in, "Head-hunters?"

"Probably. Some of the few remaining head-hunters in the world are in this district."

The party's means of travel from now on was unusual: First, Doc Savage disappeared for a time, leaving the others crouched in the jungle with eyes and supermachine pistols ready, and with stimulants and poison antidotes handy. Native head-hunters were not lads to take chances with.

Doc reappeared, and he had a huge armload of very fine fibers which he had plucked from jungle plants. The little band plaited these into thin, stout ropes, one for each man.

The task took them until noon the next day.

Then they took to the trees. Every one but Monk viewed this with great skepticism. But once aloft, they found it even easier than working through the jungle at earth level. The reason was simple:

The higher trees of this part of the jungle were huge, scrawny-leafed things, and nearly every tree had at least one branch which was like a horn in that it could be roped easily.

Doc's men had but to stand on one bough, rope a distant one, and drop a loop in their own end of the rope over another hook of a branch, then swing across. Some of them speedily perfected a way of going across upright, in a squatting position, gripping the rope on each side with their hands.

They had not gone far in this fashion before Monk made a remark.

"It looks as if some of these boughs had been used this way before," he said.

"Doubtless," Doc agreed.

"Huh?"

"This method of travel is much used in these islands," Doc replied.*

MONK proved especially adept at the new mode of travel, which was no surprise to Ham, and he found occasion to say so repeatedly and sarcastically.

The jungle below seemed to get more and more dense. It was an incredible mass. Where they could see the ground at all, it was usually covered with pools of vile green water inhabited by vicious looking water-snakes and reptiles. Travel on the ground would have been almost impossible.

Ahead, they could see a fanged mountain range, not especially high, but remarkably rugged. They were headed directly for these.

---

*Explorers have often reported the method of savage travel. The Ibilao tribesmen of the isle of Luzon are notable examples.

Doc and his aids slept that night in crude platforms which they constructed in the forks of a big tree.

A distinct *chuck!* of a noise awakened them. It was made by a short, heavy war spear which stuck in a bough of the tree.

Chapter XIV

THE STINGING BREATH

THE sun had not arrived, but there was enough pre-dawn light to show the surrounding jungle, and as Monk expressed it, "more fierce natives than you could crowd on a battleship."

The natives were little brown fellows, and they looked not greatly different from savages in other parts of the world, except perhaps they were a little more naked. The nearest were a long spear throw away. Behind them, the trees were almost bending with their fierce human freight.

As soon as Doc and his men stirred, the natives all began howling. Drums and weird-sounding reed whistles added to the uproar. Here and there was a chief or a witch doctor in a grotesque mask.

Monk drew a bead on the nearest with his machine pistol, which was loaded with "mercy" bullets.

"Careful," Doc warned.

The bronze man listened for a few moments to the shouting. He could speak innumerable languages fluently—sometimes not as fluently as he thought he should, considering the years he had spent mastering them. This one was a variation of one of the more civilized Guinea tribesman.

Doc called out in the nearest tongue he could manage, demanding what the hullabaloo meant.

The natives showed no surprise. It probably never occurred to their ignorant heads that there was any other language but their own, unless it might be the language of their witch deities.

The business of replying to Doc's question became quite a ceremony. One man would squawl for a while. Then another. And another. This continued. Then they started squawling at each other.

"What's the idea, Doc?" Monk asked. "What they talkin' over?"

"Making selections," Doc said.

"Of what?"

"Our heads," the bronze man replied quietly. "They

are aggravated because we have not enough heads to go around."

"Blazes!" Monk yelled. "Head-hunters!"

"Ham listened with interest. "Whose head are they bidding the highest for, Doc?"

"Monk's," the bronze man admitted.

"Aw-w-w!" Monk groaned.

Johnny asked uneasily, "What are they waiting for?"

"They consider that they have us trapped," the bronze man said dryly. "And they enjoy this palavering among themselves. Furthermore, there will be more light for hunting us in the jungle later in the day."

"Then what are we waiting for?"

"Shortly after the sun is up, a breeze usually starts blowing," the bronze man replied.

Johnny fumbled with his monocle, which he had preserved, although he scarcely had a piece of clothing left to which to attach the black ribbon.

"I don't see what good that will do," he said.

Doc Savage did not seem especially concerned by the fact that he and his men were surrounded by headhunters who were playing with them in their queer way. But that did not make his five aids feel any easier. They knew Doc. He would not look especially concerned if he were falling out of a plane without a parachute.

The five aids got the ammo drums for their supermachine pistols ready. There were unpleasantly few drums. Moreover, the jungle was so thick that the capsulelike mercy bullets would not be especially effective.

Came the time when the besiegers seemed to get settled the matter of who was to have whose head. They indulged in a babble of extremely loud yelling by way of warming up.

The breeze had by now piped up. It blew toward the mountains.

Doc Savage dropped several small objects into the jungle under the tree.

Then he strode out on a high, naked branch, balancing there. He called out sharply, and the great crash of his voice brought comparative silence to the jungle.

The bronze man leveled both arms in a dramatic gesture toward the distant mountains.

"We are white men who come in peace, and we are going on to those mountains," he said, in the native tongue.

The reply this got was surprising.

"No one goes to those mountains," was the substance of it. "It is forbidden by he who has all power."

Doc acted unimpressed.

"You intend to kill us?" he asked.

They shouted happily that they did.

Doc waved his arms and got some silence.

"We are not ordinary men as yourselves," he called loudly. "Should we die, our breaths would leave our bodies and go on to the mountains, and it would not be pleasant for you."

This got the head-hunters equivalent of a horse-laugh.

Doc called out again with great volume.

"In this manner it would happen," he said.

He cupped his hands about his lips, filled his chest with a great breath, and blew it noisily in the direction of the mountains.

For a moment, nothing happened. Some of the natives started cackling derisively.

Then a brown fiend shrieked, grabbed his eyes, and fell off his limb into a springy bush. Others shrieked. General bedlam seized those natives who stood between Doc's party and the mountain.

Within three or four minutes, they were as helpless as men become when dosed with tear gas.

The small objects which the bronze man had dropped had been tear-gas grenades, his aids knew by now.

Doc's voice roared over the hullabaloo.

"And our spirits would rise like black monsters to haunt you," he called. "In this fashion."

He made an elaborate gesture of plucking something out of his own head, and releasing it. Simultaneously, he opened one of the little smoke bombs.

An enormous cloud of black smoke immediately materialized above the bronze giant's head, and drifted off lazily with the wind toward the mountains.

DOC SAVAGE'S knowledge of primitive psychology was excellent, and his theatricals got the results he had aimed for.

Fight oozed out of the throng of natives. They began to howl, but there was a different tone to it, a mournful, scared quality. Weapon after weapon was thrown away.

"All right," Doc called to his aids. "They are convinced we are supernatural. We may be able to go ahead now."

They swung their rattan lariats, and began moving from tree to tree.

Doc still carried his extremely heavy metal equipment case.

As the bronze man had hazarded, no hostile move was made by the natives. Not wanting to spoil the effect created by the tear gas by themselves getting into it, the party moved to the right.

Coming to a stretch of higher ground, where the jungle was a bit too thin for fast traveling aloft, Doc and his men swung to the ground. Soon, they were surrounded by natives. The little brown fellows had discarded their weapons. They had a strange way of showing humiliation. The process seemed to be for a man to grab his own throat and go through the motions of choking himself.

This was definitely amusing to Monk. He got started chuckling, but did manage to keep his face straight.

His mirth died a gulping death when at least twenty natives suddenly surrounded them, genuflecting and choking themselves—and abruptly seized Doc Savage and his men.

"Hey!" Monk yelled. "What's the idea of this?"

Doc spoke rapidly in the dialect. He was answered.

"They are not going to harm us," the bronze man translated.

"Then what's the idea of grabbing us?"

"They are not going to let us go to the mountains," Doc said. "They are going to keep us here."

Chapter XV

THE OTHER WHITE MAN

THE native hut had one thing to recommend it: A roof. There were other things to discount that—a few overly ripe fish and some small animals hanging to the ridgepoles. This provender had been smoked for preserving purposes, but with doubtful success. There were flies in the hut. Monk was pretending to count them.

"One quintillion, seven quadrillion, two trillion——"

"Give it up," Ham requested, "or I'm going to slam you over the head so hard you'll bite your toenails."

Renny, Long Tom and Johnny also occupied the shade under the hut roof, on the side from which the wind blew. The flies were less thick there.

"Ouch!" Monk complained. "It wouldn't be so bad if these weren't man-eating flies!"

Doc Savage was nowhere in sight. His aids had pondered about where the bronze man had gone, and had decided he was moving about the village, talking to the natives, perhaps arguing.

The bronze man's helpers doubted if the arguing would help much. They had already done plenty of that, but without it getting results. They were here in the native village, prisoners, with nothing to do but stroll around and peek into the huts, a pastime that was not especially inviting, since the principal ornament in each hut was a human head, singly or in clusters.

Doc Savage appeared suddenly and called, "Ham!"

The dapper lawyer arose and accompanied the bronze man, and the others remained behind, it being obvious that Doc wanted only Ham.

Monk rolled over and frowned at Renny.

"Say, how does this thing all stack up to you?" he wanted to know.

"It has me buffaloed," Renny admitted. "Holy cow! Some of the things that have happened are impossible. That city, and that old spider-armed man, for instance. Blamed queer."

Monk nodded. "That's not all. When Doc asked these natives questions about that mountain range, and why we should not go on there, they clammed right up. Acted scared."

Long Tom put in, "Listen, if you birds haven't got any ideas, why not keep still? I can do my own puzzling."

"Yes," gaunt Johnny echoed. "Verbosity superabundantly——"

He stopped with a croak. Pointed.

"Look there!" he gulped. "There's Lupp!"

MONK, Renny and Long Tom came to their feet as if jerked by strings. They looked, and their eyes popped.

Lupp! The man who had been with Kit Merrimore, the fellow who was the real leader of their opposition. They had last seen him in the fighting aboard the *Benny Boston*. And here he was in this savage village.

Swaggering along the makeshift street area between the huts, the newcomer came. And the natives, to a man, backed away from him, took themselves by the throats, wrestled with themselves, then got down on their hands and knees.

"It's Lupp!" Renny rumbled softly.

"This is bad!" Long Tom breathed. "That fellow is obviously some kind of deity to these natives! If he sets them on us——"

The dark, muscular white man in the native street stopped and shouted what sounded like two words. The natives began to gather toward him. Lupp retreated until he stood close to the wall of the jungle, and the natives clustered before him. He lifted his arms.

Words poured from his lips. Words in the native tongue, which Monk and the others could not understand. In response, the natives chanted and throttled themselves.

Then Doc's aids got their big surprise. The man who had addressed the natives lifted his voice and spoke English.

"Doc Savage, or any of his men!" he shouted. "Can you hear me?"

"He knows we're here," Monk muttered, then howled, "We hear you, you scamp!"

"You are free to go," the man called. "I have just told the natives that they shall not prevent your departure. They were holding you because on a previous visit, I told them to prevent any white man reaching those mountains. They were obeying orders. To them, I am a powerful witch doctor. But now you can go."

The man spoke a few words to the natives, turned and disappeared into the jungle.

"Dag-gone!" Monk said, when astonishment freed his tongue. "You reckon we can walk right out of here?"

"We can try," Renny said.

They tried. And they did it. Not a war spear or poisoned arrow was lifted to stop them.

The little band penetrated about a quarter of a mile into the jungle, then stopped, their supermachine pistols in hand.

"There's some trick to this," Renny stated emphatically. "We'll wait here for Doc, then, if he don't come on, we'll go back hunting him."

"And when we find Doc, we'll trail that Lupp, Monk declared.

"You will not have to go far," a voice said almost beside them.

Doc Savage and Ham walked out of the jungle.

"You shyster!" Monk growled. "What do you mean by that?"

"I was the Lupp you saw back there," Ham vouchsafed with a smile.

Monk blinked twice, said, "I don't believe it!"

"We had better get going," Doc Savage said.

The aids climbed into the trees and used their ropes, which had been coiled about their middles. Doc still carried his heavy equipment case.

Monk declared, "I don't savvy what happened back there."

Ham said, "Simple, you Siamese gossoon. Doc got to listening and inquiring around among those natives, and he learned two men stayed with the tribesmen several months ago. Two white men. They answered the description of Lupp and that Two-bit."

"I'd hardly call Two-bit a white man," Monk said.

"That's quibbling!" Ham snapped. "Lupp and Two-bit were with those natives for a while. They *came from* the direction of those mountains ahead. When they left the tribe, they went on toward the coast.

"But before they left, Lupp had established himself as a medicine man, not a difficult thing for a clever white man to do. And Lupp had impressed upon these natives that they must not, under any condition, permit any other white men to go toward those mountains."

"But Lupp——" Monk paused and squinted intently at Ham. "Aw, bugs! I can see traces of make-up on your face! So Doc made you up to look like Lupp."

"Ham has a physical build nearest that of Lupp's," Doc admitted.

Ham added: "It was Doc done the voice imitating. I might have managed that, but I couldn't speak the darn head-hunter's language."

Big-fisted Renny, who had been silent during the recital, broke into a rumble which sounded pleased.

"We're on the right trail to the mystery!" he boomed. "We know that now!"

That very certainty which Renny mentioned injected new enthusiasm into the group's tired muscles. They made very good time through the treetops, looking back often to detect a sign of following head-hunters. They saw them.

The squat, brown natives kept some distance to the rear, so far back that they looked like monkeys in the trees. But they only followed for a few hours, then stopped and went back.

"They fear these mountains ahead," Doc Savage remarked.

"Wonder why?" Monk wanted to know.

"They call the region a name which, liberally translated, means, 'The Land of the Spook men,'" the bronze man replied. "That was about all I was able to gather."

Doc and his small group kept traveling far into the night, for the moon was bright. And only when they turned in for the night did they realize the mountains ahead were making strange sounds.

Queer sounds indeed. Rumblings, sobbings—noises that were probably distant many miles, yet which must be very loud. More striking were the sounds which came less often. They were best described as a long, gurgling *whoosh!* As if something titanic were letting out breath.

"Reminds me of the time we found some prehistoric monsters in a volcanic pit," Monk muttered uneasily. "Boy, did they show us a time!"*

Johnny polished his monocle absently.

"A monticolous terrestrial cacophony," Johnny said.

"Huh? What'd you call it?" Monk grunted.

"Mountain music," Long Tom translated dryly.

By mid-afternoon the following day, the aids began to realize what had made the noises. They climbed sharply, crossed a ridge, and descended into a low valley beyond which lay the piled masses of bare rocks that were the mountains.

All became aware of an odor. It became highly distressing.

"Calefactive thermae of earthly orgination," Johnny said.

"Blazes!" Monk groaned. "What?"

"Hot springs," Long Tom translated again. "Geysers. Look!"

Over the treetops, the associates saw a plume of steam hurl upward for a hundred feet or so, accompanied by the loud, roaring sound which they had heard the night before. In the fashion of geysers, this one hurled up water and steam for a while, then subsided.

For the first time, all realized they were headed into a region of intense volcanic activity. Geysers, boiling hot springs, great areas where the entire earth became mud that was hot enough to cook.

"Kind of like Yellowstone Park," Monk offered.

There was a difference. Yellowstone was picturesque. This region was most displeasing to the eye, and made

---

*The Land of Terror.

doubly unbearable by the brimstone smell which grew stronger and stronger.

Then the aids were pleased indeed that they had not discarded what equipment they did have, during the march. They still had the tiny gas masks which Doc Savage had perfected, and they donned them, after which the going was more bearable, except for the heat.

The heat got more intense. Earth heat. It made the sun, which they had previously thought was hot, seem almost cooling by contrast.

Time after time, Doc and his men were forced to retreat and pick another route. Since the mud lakes, almost frying hot, were covered with an innocent-looking crust, it became necessary to fling rocks ahead to test the going whenever there was the least doubt.

A moment later, they saw the spider-armed being, Goa, again.

THE creature appeared ahead of them, as on the other occasion; and waved at them, beckoning. All yelled at him, or every one but Doc did. No answer.

The aids hurried after him, and the being receded; they were beginning to have strong doubts that he was human.

Speedily Doc's aids discovered that the spider-armed man was not showing them a trail. He merely urged them to come on. And there was something pitifully pleading about his exhortations, it struck them.

"The old coot seems kinda worried," Monk took his mask off a moment to say.

Goa, it developed, could apparently pass over regions of soft mud and hot fissures where they themselves could not traverse. Doc warned of this.

"We will have to pick our trail," he said.

By noon of the following day, the bronze chief and his men had passed through the worst of the region. They reached higher ground, and the mountains shoved up around them. Sheer cliffs, for the most part.

Time after time, Doc and his aids managed to climb a few hundred yards, only to be blocked. They would go back and try a different route.

The rock higher up seemed to be veined in places with some dark formation.

The spider-armed apparition had been lost to sight for a while. But now it appeared again. For once, not ahead. To the left. They went in that direction.

Soon the group came to a stream, a creek which flowed steaming hot water. The spider-armed one went up this. Doc Savage and his aids followed. The going was easier, which meant they were not on hands and knees clawing up sheer rock faces more than half of the time.

Goa, the fantastic being with the long arms and the enveloping cloth garment, appeared to slacken his pace, so that they came nearer. Then he disappeared.

A few minutes later, Doc and his men stopped and stared.

"Holy cow!" Renny rumbled. "He musta gone into *that!*"

They had come to a cavernous opening in the face of the mountain. Out of this the boiling stream poured. Above and to the sides, the rock wall was too sheer for any man to climb.

The stone around the hole was of dark quality. The same darkish stone composed most of the mountain behind.

It was very hot, and Monk sighed and laid down his pack, including his supermachine pistol. A moment later, he reached over, picked up his gun, then gave a startled yell.

"Hey!" he squalled. "Somethin' was holdin' my gun to the ground!"

"And something," big-fisted Renny barked, "is playing the deuce with the needle of my compass!"

It was gaunt Johnny who cleared up the mystery. He pointed at the dark stone around them.

"Lodestone," he said. "The biggest deposit of the stuff, or strata of it, that I ever saw."

Monk looked relieved, bent over, and tested the pull of the black rock with his supermachine pistol. He was startled. He could free the gun only with a strong pull.

"First time I ever seen any of it this strong," Monk said.

"Lodestone," Johnny explained, "is a magnetic oxide of iron, and this particular deposit of it seems to be of high magnetic strength."

"Holy cow!" Renny interposed. "Look!" He indicated Doc Savage.

The bronze man had opened the metal equipment case which he had carried on the long trek. The case which Monk personally knew was so heavy he could hardly lift it.

Out of the case, Doc lifted six pairs of pieces of iron shaped like large flat irons. Exact copies of the strange iron implements which Ben Brasken had possessed.

He passed them out. Monk promptly lowered his to the rock underfoot, then tugged and grunted, trying to lift it against the pull of the lodestone.

"Blazes!" he complained. "What a place! You can't lay anything down!"

Big-fisted Renny peered doubtfully at the cavity out of which the boiling stream poured.

"I take it you're goin' in there, Doc?" he muttered.

"Right," the bronze man admitted.

"Why?"

By way of answering, Doc Savage called them to the mouth of the subterranean hot-water stream and showed certain scratches on the rocks which had escaped the aids' notice.

"These are several months old," he said. "But they indicate some one entered this tunnel, using iron blocks probably similar to ours."

"You think these things will support our weight?" Renny countered.

"Easily, judging from the pull outside here."

"How will we move them?"

"Slide them along. It is a crude process, but workable."

It was. Doc and his men prudently used the precaution of tying their wrists to the handles of the iron blocks before they started in. And they linked each other together with the rope, in the manner of mountain climbers, before entering.

It was not as bad as the aids had expected. The heat, terrific at first, was not so great but that they became accustomed to it.

The roof of the water-worn tunnel was smooth, hence it was possible to slide the iron blocks along by swinging and jerking. The better method was to swing up and actually shove ahead with the feet.

Yet it was probably lucky that the distance through the tunnel was not great.

Doc and his men came out at the foot of a great cliff which seemed part of the wall of a cuplike depression in the mountains. And the excitement started immediately.

Monk leveled an arm, yelled, "Our dirigible!"

Chapter XVI

THE THIRD VICTIM

THE little dirigible was perhaps half a mile distant, moored beyond a clump of trees. The back of the craft glinted in the sunlight.

This valley, or cup, crater, or whatever it was, seemed to have only a few hot springs and geysers. These appeared to be confined to the lower end, where Doc and his party had entered.

Ham breathed deeply of the air, mopped perspiration and moved away from the stream of hot water. He had managed to tug his irons free of the tunnel side, and he carried them with him. However, the rock all about —almost the entire wall around the valley—seemed to be of lodestone.

When Ham put his irons down, the magnetic force seized them, yanking him over forcibly. He sat down with a sigh.

"Of all the crazy stunts!" he groaned. "Doc, how on earth did it occur to you to make up these iron things and bring them along?"

"A natural move," Doc replied. "Ben Brasken's talk indicated they were necessary as keys."

"Ben Brasken!" Monk exploded. "If that guy swam ashore, worked through that jungle, then back, and swam around in the ocean until he met his ship—well, somebody is crazy! A thing like that couldn't be done!"

Doc Savage did not comment. The bronze man was studying the dirigible. Then he glanced at his aids, noted that it would take some time for them to recover their strength, and made a suggestion.

"While you rest, I am going ahead and look over the situation," he said.

"Go ahead," Monk groaned. "I got Charley horses in both arms."

Monk was pretty far gone when he willingly passed up a chance for action.

Doc Savage went forward. He came to a rill of fresh water, tasted it, examined it closely, even using a magnifier from his compartment vest—the most intact garment he still retained.

Convinced the striking clarity of the water did not indicate that it was poisonous, he drank. He was always suspicious of very clear water in the jungle. Fish, frogs and other creatures that roil water do not live in poison pools.

There was a cool breeze through the valley, and from the manner in which the tops of the trees bent to the southward, it was evident that this was a continuous wind. Probably it was created by the rising of air warmed by the region of geysers and hot springs.

The breeze made the going pleasant enough. The jungle was not unusually thick when Doc reached it, and he worked through it. There were many birds in the trees. Surprisingly, most of these seemed edible fowl, guineas, gamecock and species of wild chickens peculiar to the Orient. He also observed pigs, fat eating goats, and other food type animals.

Nearing the dirigible, the bronze man used caution, circling once entirely, listening often. There was no one around. He swung aboard the craft.

The airship was still in flying condition, but it had been carelessly and inexpertly handled. Many small things were broken, and a number of the special gadgets, such as the infra-light projecto-receptor for watching the earth at night with invisible light, had been taken apart by persons who did not have enough skill to get them back together. The dirigible had carried more than a dozen passengers, judging from the sleeping arrangements.

Kit Merrimore had been aboard. Doc found the innumerable bottles and boxes or beauty aids which women seemed to need in the tiny cabin which she had occupied.

The soft earth around the dirigible had been trampled a great deal. The craft was tied to trees with stout lines, and was in no danger of damage. Doc scrutinized the tracks.

The footprints were fresh. The motors bore a faint trace of warmth when he tested them.

The airship had apparently not been here long.

The footprints headed up the valley. Doc followed them.

HIS quarry had taken a straight course, which indicated they knew where they were going.

When he had covered no more than a quarter of a mile, the bronze man began hearing the shots. There was a half dozen in the first volley. After that, only a few, scattered. Doc quickened his pace.

He saw human beings. Kit Merrimore, in whipcord breeches, silk blouse and sun helmet. Lupp, dark, muscular and evil. Two-bit, the Oriental, impassively watching. And a dozen others, more or less. All were heavily armed.

They were holding two prisoners.

The man captive had the frame of a two-hundred-pounder, and probably weighed not much more than half of that. He was near fifty, and had a great deal of white hair.

The woman captive was about the same age, a tall, sturdy figure of a lady who had been pretty in her youth and was now quite handsome.

Both prisoners were whites. They were holding their hands up.

"—and you were a fool ever to come back as you have, Lupp," the man was saying. "When we found this place, it was only by the rarest accident. We all might have escaped, if it had not been for your greed. But no. You saw what was here, and you tried to take it."

Lupp laughed harshly. "It's plenty worth taking, Space!"

The white-haired man continued. "As my assistant and manager of my exploring expedition, you took advantage of my trust. It was only by double-crossing myself and my wife, leaving us behind, that you and Two-bit escaped."

Two-bit, the Celestial, squirmed uneasily and looked pained. Lupp was unaffected.

"Martin Space, the eminent explorer!" he jeered. "What the hell do you think I am? You and your kind get along on the few dimes your museums and societies hand out to you. But me, I like dough. Plenty of dough. I thought I was gonna get it, only they up and repealed prohibition in the States. Then I ran onto my big chance here. What kind of a sucker do you take me for?"

"You're not a sucker," replied the white-haired Space. "You are as unprincipled a devil as was spawned."

Lupp laughed again. "Now that we've got that settled, we'll proceed."

"And what do you think you are going to do?" Space asked calmly.

"Get rid of you and your wife permanently," Lupp said.

"Murder?"

"It's only murder when you get caught. There's not much chance of that."

Lupp cocked the large revolver he was carrying and raised it.

"Lupp!" Kit Merrimore cried out, in horror.

Lupp half lowered his gun and looked at the young woman who was known around New York as a thrill-hunter with too much money.

"What'd you think we would do?" he demanded.

Kit Merrimore gasped. "When you came to me in New York to finance this thing, you told me there would be no killing, and that you would rescue Martin Space and his wife!"

Lupp laughed. "I've changed my ideas."

"You'll change them again!" the young woman snapped. "You are not going to murder these people or anybody else!"

Lupp nodded at his men. Several lifted their weapons.

"We're going ahead with it," Lupp said grimly. "And let me tell you something else! I've been making a play for you ever since we started this thing, and not been getting any place. From now on, that is going to be different, too!"

Kit Merrimore bent forward a little. She showed her teeth, and it was not a smile.

"You touch me," she said too calmly, "and I'll kill you if it's the last thing I ever do!"

It was not a loud declaration, but it had a quality in it that caused Lupp to move back a step, as if he had just missed being bitten by a poisonous snake. He recovered immediately.

"Grab her!" he ordered his men.

Four men sprang for Kit Merrimore. She tried to whip a small gun out, but did not quite succeed. She fired at one of the men from her pocket, and the bullet damaged his leg slightly, causing him to emit an ear-splitting howl. Then they got the young woman's gun and held her.

Lupp looked her up and down evilly, but at the same time he seemed to be thinking. He had evidently observed Kit Merrimore enough to realize she would be dangerous as long as she was alive. Too dangerous, he must have thought, for he shrugged.

"Put her with Space and his wife," Lupp ordered. "Women will be a dime a dozen when we get back outside."

They shoved Kit Merrimore toward the explorer and his wife.

"You're going to kill me?" Kit Merrimore demanded.

"Hell, yes," Lupp said frankly. "I'm afraid of you."

The men stepped back from Kit Merrimore and the two Spaces. They got their guns ready.

Martin Space said desperately, "Goa is my friend now! You will never live to leave this——"

"Give it to them!" Lupp rapped. "We'll take care of Goa and the rest of——"

He did not finish it. The rock made an almost metallic noise hitting the side of his head.

HAVING thrown the rock, Doc Savage lost no time. He heaved erect, charged. During the excitement connected with Kit Merrimore's seizure, he had crawled close.

He hit two men, lifted them, flung them into two others. All four went down. Doc had a smoke bomb in one hand. He flung it to the earth. It bloomed a black mushroom, and an instant later no one was very sure where anybody else was.

Doc Savage, who had started quite effectively, was himself somewhat out of luck, because he made a few hearty swings at the spot where Lupp had been, but Lupp had moved, fortunately for him. The bronze man finally connected with some one else, and knocked him completely out of the smoke cloud.

The smoke had a certain stinging effect on the lungs and eyes, not enough to blind, or even make one cough, if one used self-control. The sting was vastly disturbing to those who did not know much about it, for they immediately thought it was gas, probably poison.

Doc changed position, found Martin Space and his wife, whose feet were tied. He picked them up bodily.

Some one said, "No, you don't!" and hit him three times about as fast as he had ever been hit before. It was Kit Merrimore.

Doc said, "Stop that!" and she stopped. Furthermore, she was of some aid in getting out of the mêlée, to the extent that she tripped some one.

They got out of the smoke cloud.

"Run!" Doc said, and they ran.

The man whom Doc had knocked out of the smoke was sitting on the ground and he saw them.

"Here they go!" he began to bawl. *"Here* they go!"

That was the wrong thing from his standpoint. He should have said, *"There* they go." His friends ran for his voice, and by that time Doc Savage had steered his party around to the other side of the smoke cloud—*and back into it.*

Going back into the smoke was a smooth move. The clearing was one of size, and the group would probably have been shot full of holes had they tried to get across it.

As it was, the enemy thought by some miracle Doc and the prisoners had traversed the distance to the jungle, and immediately began to shoot the luxuriant tropical growth full of holes, to the immense distress of wild guineas and not-so-wild goats.

Meanwhile, Doc Savage and his party simply kept

in the smoke cloud and walked along with it—the bronze man's judgment of the wind speed was nice— as the breeze swept it to the opposite side of the clearing. Once under cover, Kit Merrimore took off her nice, shiny, but stiff and clumsy boots, after which it was remarkable with what silence she could move.

The party traversed all of a half mile without anybody saying anything but, "Watch that dry stick," or "It looks more open over here," and such stuff.

At the end of the half mile, Kit Merrimore stopped, looked Doc Savage up and down, and shook her head.

"What a prize one I've been," she said.

SOME men might have agreed with her, but Doc Savage had acquired restraint, and moreover, was afraid of women. If not afraid, he at least considered them too difficult, one never knowing what they would do.

Kit Merrimore began, "They played me for a sucker to finance them. Lupp is a former gangster and bootlegger, and when he needed men for this job, he gathered up his old associates; but they did not have money enough to buy a plane or finance a trip here. So they used me, telling me——"

Doc told her he had heard all that, thus heading off a redundant explanation.

"Well," the girl said, "there is a lot you don't know about this place and what it is."

Doc told her he had formed some ideas and left the impression that he was interested in knowing how close his guessing had been.

"But Lupp and the gang will hunt for us," he said. "And we are too close to them."

The band appreciated that.

"What is the best direction for safety?" Doc asked.

"To Ost," Martin Space said. "It is at the far end of the valley. You cannot see it from here."

Doc indicated they would go in that direction. They did.

Kit Merrimore reminded, "Your men. What about them? Or are they with you?"

"They can take care of themselves about as well as any five men alive," Doc said.

Then he was reminded of something else which would likely interest Monk and Ham:

"What about the pig and the what-is-it?" he asked.

"So that's what you call that thing that looks like a monkey," the girl said. "Well they must be around in the jungle somewhere. They never did take to Lupp, and both pets ran when Lupp seized Martin Space and his wife."

Martin Space said, "We saw the dirigible land, and ran to meet the crew. We did not dream it was Lupp."

Doc asked, "What about the Ostians?"

"I guess they saw the dirigible, too," Martin Space decided. "But they would fuss around some before they started to see what it was. Have to consult old Goa and their other yogis first, you know. They'll be along in time."

"On our side?" Doc asked.

"Oh, definitely," Martin Space declared. "They are my friends."

About this time, men began walking out of the jungle around them. They were grotesque fellows with incredibly long arms, big heads, bodies which were mostly belly and legs which did not amount to much. They were all blue. Some were more blue than others.

Each man carried a short stick made of some dark wood resembling mahogany and about as long as a walking stick. To one end of each of these sticks was affixed a noose made out of stuff which resembled braided fiddlestrings.

They showed every indication of intending to lasso Doc and the others with these unique weapons.

Chapter XVII

GOA

DOC SAVAGE leaped backward a few paces, picked up a long branch which had fallen from a tree and took a swat at the nearest blue Ostian. The fellow got out from under with the nimbleness of a fly, using his long arms. Doc whacked and poked and temporarily discouraged the assault.

"So they are your friends!" Kit Merrimore told Martin Space dryly.

Space said, as if it explained everything, "These are some low-caste Ostians."

"High or low, they mean business," the girl declared. "What is the difference?"

"Ignorance," Space said. "These chaps are dumb, frenziedly given to superstitious beliefs. They think white people are evil spirits or devils, who will do them no good."

"If they knew the history of American Indians," Kit Merrimore declared, "they would know they weren't so far wrong."

Doc made a few more passes with his long stick. The twig was thicker than his wrist, and the Ostians appeared to marvel greatly at the kind of man who could wield such a tree as if it were really light. This held them back. Then they came closer.

They now used some of the strategy which American Indians found rather effective on covered-wagon trains. They circled, yelling, jumping up and down, and occasionally jumping at Doc or one of his group.

They held their sticks with the nooses on the ends ready.

"This is the craziest thing I ever dreamed of!" Kit Merrimore gasped. "I'll bet an audience would kill itself laughing if they saw this on a screen!"

"The audience," Martin Space said, "wouldn't be able to feel those nooses like we will."

"You mean they'll choke us?" the girl cried.

"It's their religion," Space said, talking like a scientist telling a student a bug had five legs. "They believed they will go to hell if they kill anybody or anything. But if they tie something around your neck and you suffocate, they figure you just died.

"They don't understand what suffocation is, so they don't believe it is anything they caused. It's a custom throughout the South Seas, for that matter. Why, the natives on many islands choke a chicken instead of ringing its neck when they want one for supper. In other words——"

"That's enough words!" groaned the young woman who liked her thrills.

The words were hardly out when she followed them with an *"Eeek!"* An Ostian had lassoed her. He gave the stick a yank, the noose tightened more, and punchhunter Kit Merrimore began to act like a chicken which had suddenly lost its head.

Every Ostian low-caste emitted a brother-greeting howl and sprang to the attack. Doc instinctively felt of his pocketed vest, but he was out of the smoke bombs which had proved so effective.

A supermachine pistol would have helped the situation materially, but Doc never carried one of the weapons himself, feeling that carrying any sort of firearm made the carrier too dependent upon the weapon. This was not the first time the theory had looked bad in practice.

A lasso got Doc's arm. The blue human spider who held it started to yank, but was himself yanked forward against Doc's fist. A man rushed in—he probably did not realize just how foolish he was being—and grabbed Doc. The blue devil was strong in the arms, but weak in the legs. Before Doc could get rid of him, another was on them.

Doc reached for his tear-gas capsules. He had only one, and he had intended to save it if possible. It did not look as if it were possible.

There was a sound as if some one had broken the smallest and tightest string on a piano.

An Ostian fell over with one of his eyes shot out.

THE crash of the rifle reached them an instant later. It was followed by more bullets and more crashes. Some of the bullets missed, but some didn't.

Doc did not need Kit Merrimore's, "Lupp!" to know what was happening.

"Run!" the bronze man ordered.

They had no trouble doing that. The Ostians had stopped everything else and were looking at each other. When one of their number would fall over with a bullet in him, they would look at him with their mouths open, and even walk over and peer down at him, kick him, and cackle at him, asking him what kind of silly game the man was trying to play.

It was pitiful because they did not know what a rifle was and did not realize they were being killed.

Doc whirled and yelled at them in a dialect which he believed was, of all those he knew, closest to the one they spoke.

"Run!" he told them. "A strange devil is killing you!"

The dialect which he used happened to be an Indo-China tribal one. And Indo-China was not very near to New Guinea, unless two thousand five hundred miles could be called near.

The Ostians paid no attention to the yell, but kept on acting like chickens when another chicken is shot. They understood what Doc had shouted, but their re-action was the wrong one.

Any time their deities sent a devil which squeaked and banged to kill them, they probably needed killing, one yelled. This last was what Martin Space gasped out as the group plunged into the jungle. He could understand the tongue.

A number of bullets smashed through the foliage as Lupp and his men fired.

"Go on!" Doc said.

"But you?" Kit Merrimore gasped.

"Go on!" Doc said, and there was something in his voice that shut the young woman up and made her run on with the Spaces. And Kit Merrimore had not taken an order from anybody in a long time. When she did think of that, it made her mad, and she stopped.

"Come on!" Martin Space said.

"Nobody is going to order me around!" said Kit Merrimore. "That big fellow is too free with telling people what to do."

Martin Space then demonstrated that he was a judge of character.

"You are a young woman without much judgment," he told Kit Merrimore. "And that man is Doc Savage, who was just beginning to be known as one of the most remarkable men who ever lived, about the time I started this New Guinea exploration which brought me here."

"If you were a women, I'd slap you!" Kit Merrimore said angrily, not being used to being told the truth.

Mrs. Space, who had said almost nothing up to this point, said, "I'm a woman, and I'd love for you to slap me. I'd paddle you good!"

Kit Merrimore got madder and madder and finally burst out laughing.

"Let's run," she said.

Doc Savage had turned back for two reasons, any one of which would have been enough: He wanted to save the lives of the silly blue Ostians. And he wanted to get Lupp and his men off the trail of Martin Space, his wife and Kit Merrimore. The same move would accomplish both purposes. He made it.

He simply showed himself to Lupp's gang. The latter started yelling and shooting. Doc got behind a big tree near which he had foresightedly looked for. He got down low enough so that the irregularities of the earth sheltered him, and left, making a plain trail.

A pack of redbone foxhounds would not have made more noise folling the trail than Lupp and his men made. They must have brought plenty of ammunition along, because they were free with it. None of the slugs would have hit a quarry who used ordinary sense, and Doc evaded them easily, keeping well ahead.

Lupp's men began to get discouraged. And possibly a little scared. By now they knew the bronze man could pass muster as a blend between a ghost, a magician and a bobcat. He was nobody to be loose in the same woods with if he didn't like you.

Doc egged them on a little with an old bobwhite trick. He fell down when he came to a soft spot where the marks would show, and dragged his legs as if he were wounded.

The howl that went up when the pursuers came to that place made every one happy.

When Doc had led them over to the northern wall of cliffs, about a mile, he took to the treetops, swung from branch to branch with an agility that seemed uncanny unless one had studied the tricks of circus acrobats, and left the pursuers to poke around the terminus of a trail abruptly ended, and eventually to start calling each other names that meant stupid.

By that time, Doc had found Kit Merrimore, Martin Space and the latter's wife. Kit Merrimore had a sweet smile for the bronze man.

Kit Merrimore was a remarkable young woman in that she could carry her peeves when the danger and mystery around her would have made another weak with unease. She had decided to use her feminine weapons on Doc. Get him agog about her. Then squash him plenty.

She did not know Doc very well yet, or she would not have wasted time with that idea.

"You really think it is safe to go to this Ost?" Doc asked.

"Indeed I do," Martain Space said. "Goa is my friend."

"So were those Ostians back there," Kit Merrimore remembered aloud dryly.

WHEN the party got their first glimpse of Ost, they all stood still and nobody spoke or hardly breathed. They did that for almost five minutes.

People do that when they see the Grand Canyon.

Ost was black. So shiny black that it almost hurt the eyes. The pyramids seemed to be made of stone, and looked as if one great slab had been placed on top of a greater one, then a smaller one on the very top, to make each house. That was only the effect, though, for the slabs were doubtless rooms, or floors of rooms.

Every building was made with mathematical precision, and they were arrayed in a neat semicircle—a letter C of buildings with the opening of the C against a tremendous overhanging cliff. A wall connected the buildings.

The really gigantic size of this cliff, and the fact that it overhung hundreds of feet, did not become fully apparent until later.

It was vaguely like the city of Ost which had been seen at sea. Yet different. That had been an outline, vague, like a phosphorescent photographic print, underexposed.

Martin Space speared out an arm.

"The temple of Goa the Mighty," he said.

There was no mistaking what he meant—the upsidedown building. It was like the others, a pyramid of black stone. But it was upside down, against the underside of the great cliff which was such an overhanging mass.

The amazing structure, because of its incredible position, looked larger than some of the others, but probably was not.

"The black rock is all magnetic iron oxide," Doc Savage said.

Martin Space nodded. "Commonly called lodestone. The mineral of nature which attracts metal like a magnet."

"Whew!" gasped Kit Merrimore. "What a relief! I was just beginning to think we were in a land where the natural course of things had reversed themselves. The cliff is loadestone, and that temple or whatever you called it is lodestone, too, and they attract each other. That is why the temple sticks to the underside of the cliff that way."

Martin Space nodded again, then added, "But let me warn you."

"What about?"

"You are going to find some things in Ost that are much harder than that to explain," Space said. "But let me warn you now. Everything you see here, which may seem impossible, can be explained by modern science. Everything! Remember that and it may literally save your reason."

"You sound," Kit Merrimore said, "as if this was quite a place."

"The place is not as unusual as the beings you will find here," Space replied.

Chapter XVIII

SIEGE

CULTIVATED fields were around the party as they went forward toward Ost. It was an intensive kind of cultivation. First, there was a wall across the valley, a low wall inset along the top with pointed stakes. A fence to keep back the goats and other semi-domesticated animals.

Doc, observing closely, noted that they scaled the wall without trouble. At intervals along the fence poles atop which were contraptions turned by the wind and which flapped bits of leather and made noises calculated to frighten out of his wits any crow or buzzard. Scattered through the fields were other such scarecrows.

Doc, observing closely, noted that the parts of these scarecrows which turned were inscribed with what were apparently prayer symbols similar to the *"Om mani padme hum,"* of the Tibetans. Each revolution of the wheel was doubtless construed as offering a prayer for the wheel's owner and builder. Thus the wheels served both as prayer mediums and as warnings to the birds.

The fields were as intensively cultivated as hotbeds or greenhouses. Each patch was surrounded by a stone retaining wall, and there were stone-walled ditches, some filled with water for irrigating.

Everything stood as if work had been suddenly interrupted. Here and there were baskets, still filled with fertilizer, and hoes and leveling rakes had been dropped in the fields.

"They fled to the temple when they saw the dirigible," said Martin Space.

The black pyramids and connecting wall of Ost grew larger—at least that was the effect—as Doc and the others approached. The great ledge shoved out toward them, and it was not apparent that the gigantic shelf of stone literally overhung at least half of the strange metropolis of Ost itself.

"Whew!" breathed Kit Merrimore. "Are these inhabitants of Ost invisible or something?"

When Martin Space did not reply, the young woman stared at him and her lips came apart and her eyes got wide.

"Are they?" she gasped.

"Oh, not exactly anything like that," Martin Space muttered. "But—well, I am afraid you will begin to think your mind is going haywire before long."

The black wall connecting the pyramid was too high for any man to jump, even with the aid of a pole, and was glass smooth, so that there was no climbing it.

But at one point there was an opening, rectangular, evidently arranged to be closed by a sliding panel of the stone. Doc Savage and the others passed through.

"I do not know what will happen," Martin Space said. "But keep your heads."

Kit Merrimore looked around when they were through the aperture in the wall. There was no one in sight. Ahead stretched a flat area, and on either side was the ring of strange pyramidical houses. There was one very striking thing about the whole picture: The incredible neatness.

There were no small objects about. No baskets. No implements, vessels or trinkets. There was no dust or dirt, even; not a single article of clothing could be seen anywhere.

There was no sound. Only the shiny blackness of the unusual lodestone of which everything was made. And the cliff, a looming black silence overhead, with the upside-down building under it. Stillness——

Mrs. Space said, "Goa—he always—I feel, when I see him—as the Egyptians must have felt when they saw the waters part for the Israelites."

Martin Space, as if the words had been all that was needed to give him a final shove, stopped.

He said, "Mr. Savage, perhaps I should try to make some things clear before we go any farther."

DOC SAVAGE came to a halt. For a moment, the weird silence seemed as real as a monster.

Doc Savage said, "These people are of Hindu descent, the original followers of the yogi beliefs, and have been at it for centuries."

Martin Space did not seem surprised. He nodded.

"You have an analytical and reasoning mind," he said. "I hoped you would realize that what you will see here is real, and absolutely possible. You are right about these people of Ost being of Hindu and Yogi descent."

"You know the history of the Ostians?" Doc queried.

"They once populated a city in what I presume is now Indo-China," Space replied. "Whether it is the lost city which was found in the Indo-China jungles a few years ago, I do not know. You will recall that such a city was found, and no one has as yet been able to explain what became of the people who built it and vanished centuries ago."*

Doc said, "That is true."

"The Ostians were driven out of their original city by a plague," Space continued. "Their yogis, or medicine men, got them here, to this place. It must have been a terrible trip, but boats were known in that day, although it was long before the time of Christ.

"They reached this valley and the magic black mountain, and stayed here because of the mountain. You and I know the mountain is only magnetic iron oxide, or iron oxide magnetized by the earth itself. But the Ostians considered it a magic mountain."

"They have been here since?" Doc asked.

"Oh, yes. Remember, I said they were followers of the yogi belief from the first? Yogis are believers in few comforts for their bodies and much deep thinking. A great yogi would spend his time in sitting and thinking about things and the world and the mysteries of life, instead of trying to make a lot of money."

"Sort of the opposite of the way things go in New York," Kit Merrimore said dryly.

"Twenty-three or twenty-four hundred years of thought and reflection explains what you are going to see soon, and some of what you have already experienced," Martin Space finished. "Come. We will speak to Goa."

---

*Such a city was found in Indo-China by explorers, and movie patrons may recall having seen motion pictures which were made of the fantastic place and later exhibited over the United States.

He walked to a spot under the strange temple hanging from the underside of the cliff. As they drew near, a stout cord with a knot every foot or so came snaking down from the upside-down temple.

Goa descended the cord.

THERE was nothing new about the appearance of Goa. Doc Savage and his aids had seen, apparently, the fellow before. The master yogi—that was what he turned out to be—was the spider-armed fellow who had appeared in the jungle and urged them on toward Ost.

His age was undoubtedly beyond seventy, and he was clad only in an enormously long red cloth which he had wrapped around and around his person, tucking the end in. His arms were strong, judging from the easy manner in which he descended the line. When he spoke, it was in excellent English, although there was nothing Caucasian about the cast of his features.

"You will climb the rope, and at the top you will find a spot where you can talk," he said.

Doc Savage tested the line. It seemed solid. Martin Space went up. He seemed to have had practice, for he had no trouble. His wife, a muscular woman, also mounted. Then Kit Merrimore, and finally, Doc Savage. They left the remarkable creature, Goa, at the foot of the rope.

Doc Savage swung through a hole into a square black room which was absolutely bare and lighted only by such illumination as was reflected up through the hole. The room had no other opening.

Kit Merrimore looked down at Goa standing at the foot of the rope.

"He gives me the creeps," she said.

The next instant she jumped and cried out. Goa was suddenly standing almost beside her. *And he had not climbed the line!*

Kit Merrimore blinked at him. "Why—why—you must be twins!"

"I have been standing here all the time," Goa said calmly.

Kit Merrimore looked suddenly indignant. She opened her mouth, and it was plain to be seen she was going to state in no uncertain terms that she knew when she was being kidded and didn't like it.

Doc Savage stopped her.

"Goa is a master of self-projection," the bronze man said.

The young woman obviously knew what that meant. She stared at Doc as if about to call him a liar, then thought better of it, moistened her lips and said, "I— well, I'm just a bit too modern for that. There is no such thing!"

"On the contrary," the bronze man replied. "You have just seen proof of it. Goa stood here, yet we saw him down there at the front of the rope."

"There is some trick to it!" the girl snapped.

The bronze man shook his head: "It is real enough in this case, apparently. Just how it is accomplished is beyond my present ability to explain. At any rate, it is known the brain definitely does set up tiny magnetic fields, and that nervous impulses are probably electrical in nature, so it is not absolutely impossible that the brain does send out impulses just as a radio station sends out ether impulses. Not the same kind, naturally."

"I'll be darned if I can believe it," said Kit Merrimore.

"Myself and my men saw Goa plainly on the seacoast many miles from here, and later in the jungles," Doc explained. "And you will recall that many sailors saw this city of Ost, a likeness of which Goa must have projected by mental power."

"All right!" snapped Kit Merrimore. "That's enough. I don't believe any of it. I won't believe anything that anybody can't explain to me so I can understand!"

"Science has been unable to explain many of the mysteries of the Orient," Doc Savage reminded.*

---

*Among the mysterious feats of Hindu fakirs which science has been unable to explain is the one where the yogi floats unsuspended and unsupported in mid-air before the eyes of the observers. For many years, travelers have reported witnessing this impossible feat. For years, it was claimed by scientists that hypnotism was used. But within recent months *actual pictures* have been taken of the subject suspended in mid-air. Such pictures appeared in the *Illustrated London News* among other publications, and were reprinted in some magazines in the United States. While it may be possible

Goa said calmly, "There are more important things to discuss than what I can and cannot do."

"What?" Doc Savage asked.

"Not a pleasant subject," the strange creature replied. "Death."

THE bronze man did not change expression, but Kit Merrimore blanched a little.

"Whose death?" Doc asked.

Martin Space answered that question. "My own and my wife's," he said. "And now, probably the lives of this young lady, yourself and your men."

Goa nodded. "I might add, my own as well."

Martin Space looked at the strange blue, long-armed old fellow in red.

"I am sorry, Goa," Space muttered. "You befriended me, and used your mental powers in an attempt to summon help from the outer world to take myself and my wife back to civilization."

Doc Savage listened with interest to this.

"You know a sailor named Ben Brasken?" Doc asked Goa.

"No," the old man replied, "except that I read your mind after a fashion. That is one of my powers, as you would call it. I see by your thoughts that Ben Brasken is some one who caught my projection of the city."

Kit Merrimore gasped, "Then Ben Brasken didn't come here?"

Doc replied, "He did not. He could not have, because it was physically impossible, and Ben Brasken was no yogi. What happened was this: Ben Brasken had a dreamer's mind, and was more receptive to Goa's thought projection than the other sailors on the *Benny Boston*. Ben Brasken was put into a state of coma, so greatly was his mind affected.

---

to hypnotize an individual and make him think he was seeing something which was not happening, hypnotizing a camera is something else again.

For years, skeptics have laughed off these impossible feats of the yogis by saying that it was hypnotism since a camera photograph showed nothing. But the above instance definitely refutes this contention.

—Kenneth Robeson.

"He crept off to a recess in the ship, probably one where he was in the habit of going when he wanted to be alone. He remained there for days, not entirely himself mentally, under the spell of Goa's projected thoughts all the time. He made those iron blocks while under the spell." The bronze man paused and glanced at Goa.

"Naturally, I included instructions in how to get here in my projected thoughts," Goa said. "I also sent out mental pictures of Martin Space and his wife."

Doc Savage nodded. "There is one other thing which Ben Brasken mentioned that you have not explained."

"What?"

"Something that Ben Brasken called a terrible fear."

THE strange silence was no longer outside. As the party had entered Ost, the sinister quiet had been perhaps the most striking thing. But now there were noises, low calling for the most part, but occasionally a sharper shout. And as moments dragged on, there were more and more of the shouts.

Goa seemed interested in the noises more than he was in the conversation they were having.

"The fear?" he said vaguely. "Oh, that! Perhaps Martin Space had best explain it."

Martin Space nodded. "Goa is my friend, you understand. He is the only friend I have here, or that any white man has, really. It was different when we first came, when we first stumbled on this place by accident and slid down into the valley with ropes. Some of them were friendly to us, then. But Lupp killed some of them when he escaped."

"I did not know that," Doc said.

Space nodded. "Only Goa's warnings saved my life then."

The muttering below was louder, more ominous.

Doc Savage asked Goa, "What makes your beliefs differ from those of the other Ostians?"

Old Goa shrugged. "They do not believe as I," he said. "Thinking is hard work, and for the last generation or two, it has rather stopped. I am the last of the great thinkers. The human brain is like what you call a muscle, and if it is not used, it falls off in strength. As for the question of the life of this man Martin Space— why should he die?"

There was really no reason.

Doc said, "Lupp came back."

"We were afraid he would," Space muttered.

"Why did he return?"

Space looked at Goa. The queer old fellow shrugged in a perfectly human way.

"No harm in telling him," he said. "The real harm was done when Lupp found out about it."

Space told Doc. "When these people left their ancient home, they brought along the accumulations of generations of wealth. At the expense of sounding trite, I will say that they have gold and jewels such as you never dreamed existed. You know that even to-day some of the greatest collections of hoarded wealth are to be found in India. The instinct to hoard must be a racial one."

Kit Merrimore said, "Lupp told me he saw a pair of cut diamonds as large as his fists!"

"The eyes of an ancient image of some kind," Space nodded. "Such huge jewels were almost invariably used for such purposes."

There was a sharp cackle of shouts below. They had an angry imperativeness.

Goa went to the floor aperture and stared downward. They babbled up at him.

Goa looked at the bronze man and the others.

"It is too bad you are not up to the task of self-projection," he said softly. "If so, you might make them think you were elsewhere. I, myself, may be able to escape them in that fashion."

Doc Savage went to the aperture and looked down. The area immediately below was blue with the spider-armed men. They were armed with their queer sticks and nooses, and with large blocks of wood, bundles of reeds, and jars which seemed to contain an oil of some kind.

"They look as if they meant business," Kit Merrimore said.

OLD Goa, who talked as if he were one of them in spite of his amazing appearance, said, "Lupp and his men killed some of them, and they have decided to kill every white man in the valley. After all, it is a very simple conclusion for them to reach. And not a bad one."

"They will have their difficulties when they tackle Lupp," Doc Savage said, "Lupp is armed with some very modern machine guns and military equipment."

Kit Merrimore made her jaw firm.

"If you think they're going to bump *us* off easily, you've got another guess coming!" she snapped. She whirled, eyed old Goa. "What is there around here to fight with?"

Goa shrugged. "Nothing."

Kit Merrimore squinted at him. "Look here! You sound phony to me! You are supposed to be some kind of a yogi or medicine man who spent his life sitting here meditating. That don't ring right, because you speak English as if you had been throwing it around all your life!"

Goa shrugged again, spread his hands.

"My friend Martin Space has been here a long time, and Lupp and the Chinaman, Two-bit, were also here, and from them I learned the tongue," he said. "It does not take me long to learn things. My brain is a storehouse which I keep well in order."

A puff of smoke drew the party's attention to the opening again. The Ostians had made a great pile of timbers, kindling and tinder below, had dumped their oil on the whole, and some one had come running with a hot coal. The mass was blazing up. They were bringing more fuel.

Space swallowed, said with an effort, "Trying to suffocate us!" and looked at his wife.

"It's all right, Martin," his wife said.

Kit Merrimore declared, more as a statement of fact than in a panic, "I'm not ready to die yet by a long shot!"

Old Goa sighed.

"I think there is a part of man which never dies," he said. "I confess a great curiosity to find out about that, yet I am a bit reluctant to be shoved into taking the step."

Chapter XIX

THE REST OF THE VICTIMS

Doc Savage's five associates were still at the mouth of the underground boiling-hot stream by which they had entered the valley. The bronze man had told them to wait there. They had waited. About long enough, they were thinking.

Renny stood up and blocked and unblocked his huge fists.

"Holy cow!" he rumbled. "Something has gone wrong. And I'm in favor of using our judgment."

The others agreed. That was the usual procedure. Orders from the bronze man were to be obeyed, but not if their better judgment told them there was some good reason why they should not be.

The shots they had heard much earlier had impressed them as being reason enough.

"We should 'a' gone to find out what that shooting was about right off the bat," Monk muttered.

The party headed for the dirigible. Having rested, they felt much better. The heavy iron contraptions by which they had entered the valley were difficult to carry, so they buried them at the foot of a prominent tree, and hid the spot well.

Approaching near the dirigible, Doc's men discovered three of Lupp's men guarding it. The trio were much too alert to be captured without a noise. They might easily be winged with the machine pistols and mercy bullets, but that would mean a racket, too.

"I got an idea," Monk whispered.

"Treat it gently," Ham snapped. "It's in a strange place. What is it?"

"Take the carburetors or somethin' off the airship, you clothes-horse shyster, so the thing won't fly," Monk said.

Ham gritted his teeth to show what he thought of that.

"I suppose them three guards won't have anything to say about it?" he sneered.

AT this point, two more men appeared out of the jungle and walked toward the three guards watching the dirigible. There was a short conference, then the two climbed into the motor gondolas, which were really compartments entirely contained within the craft. There was a clinking of tools on metal. The men climbed out again in about five minutes.

They carried the injection jets, very essential parts of the special Diesel motors with which the craft was powered. The Diesels did not have carburetors, as Monk now recollected.

"Blazes!" the homely chemist gritted. "They thought of it ahead of us!"

Lupp's men now walked away from the dirigible, heading up the valley. They carried the jets, which were not heavy.

"I'll be superamalgamated!" bony Johnny muttered. "An obreptitious reconnoiter is propitious."

"Eh?" Monk said.

Long Tom translated, "I guess he means we better trail 'em."

They did that. It was not difficult. Monk, as if he had something he wanted to think over, dropped behind.

Perhaps fifteen minutes later, the others suddenly discovered Monk was no longer with them. He had disappeared.

"Do you suppose something could have happened to him?" Ham gasped.

The stark anxiety in Ham's voice was surprising in view of the things he had been telling Monk about the latter and his ancestors and how little he—Ham—would care if Monk fell into one of the sulphur-exuding volcanic cracks they had passed enroute, which would be only a sample, Ham claimed, of where Monk was eventually going, anyhow.

Ham, when Monk came stalking out of the jungle a bit later, flew into a rage again, however.

"We thought you had got killed," Ham gritted, "and had just stopped to cheer!"

Monk grinned amiably. The homely chemist was carrying some metal objects.

"The airship won't fly without these, either," he said, and exhibited them.

He had removed certain very essential gears from the Diesels.

"Now I gotta find a place to bury 'em," he said.

He looked around. Immediately, his eyes protruded.

"Glory be!" Monk gulped.

The Chinaman, Two-bit, had come out of the jungle and was watching them.

MONK, who looked as clumsy as a Missouri snapping turtle, produced his supermachine pistol with astonishing speed.

"Start somethin', heathen!" he squeaked. "I think I could die happy, once I got to pepper you good!"

Two-bit grinned at them as if they were his very dear friends.

"Velly happy see you fella," he said.

Monk and the others exchanged startled looks.

"Me look all ovel hellee fo' you fella," Two bit explained blandly.

Monk growled suspiciously, and said, "There's a Celestial in the woodpile here somewhere!"

While Two-bit stood smiling happily at Doc's men, and they stood waiting for whatever to happen that was going to happen—nothing would really have surprised them—the pig, Habeas Corpus, and the what-is-it, Chemistry, came out of the jungle and stood at Two-bit's side.

Two-bit bent over and scratched each animal.

"Velly nice hog and velly nice funny monk," he said.

Monk and Ham gave signs of having been struck dead where they stood.

"They likee me," Two-bit explained.

"Habeas!" Monk yelled. "Ain't you got no pride a-tall!"

"Shut up, you dope!" Renny thumped softly. "They could hear that yell back in San Francisco!"

"This is a yelling matter!" Monk gurgled. "Ham, that danged flea-carrier of yours has plum corrupted my hog!"

"My—my——" Ham sputtered his indignation. "If there was any corrupting done, your hog——"

"Missy Kit Mellimole likee two animals, too," Two-bit offered.

"There!" Monk croaked. "That's what caused it. That danged girl!"

Long Tom strode forward alertly and addressed Two-bit.

"Just what are you doing here, fellow?" the electrical wizard demanded.

Two-bit said, "You fella make mistake about me all along."

"Yeah?"

"Me fliend of Maltin Space," said Two-bit.

NATURALLY, none of Doc's associates believed Two-bit. and since nature seems to have endowed each Oriental with a poker face, they were not much more certain after they had questioned him closely.

Two-bit, in answer to their queries, maintained he had been a faithful servant to explorer Martin Space throughout, and had joined Lupp only with the idea of getting to civilization and bringing help back to get Martin Space and his wife.

Two-bit blandly explained that the reason Lupp had returned to he valley was to get the store of ancient wealth which the Ostians had brought here from their original dwelling place.

"The story is hokum!" Monk declared.

"It tluth," Two-bit declared.

"It's a lie! You had plenty of chances in the United States to escape from Lupp and tell your story."

"You no savvy," Two-bit complained. "It do me no good to escape, because only Lupp know how find this place again. Me, I tly and tly to steal papel with location on it, but Lupp keep it hid some place all time."

The bronze man's aids put some sharp queries to Two-bit about this, but did not shake him. Even Ham, an expert at such stuff because of his legal training, could not make the Oriental admit he was lying.

They gave it up in disgust.

"We'll take him along and go see what's in the upper end of the valley," Monk said.

Doc's men started forward, after searching Two-bit

and finding a revolver on him. They came to a well-worn trail, headed along it.

Two-bit immediately balked.

"Not this way!" the Oriental objected. "You fella fall in tlap!"

"Yeah?" Monk inquired.

"Lupp fella watch this tlack," Two-bit explained.

Monk thought that over, then grinned thinly.

"So that's it!" the homely chemist growled. "Listen, fellows! Lupp sent this rice-eater to steer us wrong! Probably he's got a trap set, and Two-bit, here, wants to lead us into it. What do you think?"

"I say follow the trail," Renny rumbled.

The others agreed, and they followed the trail.

Two-bit lost his temper and said some rather expressive words which he must have picked up around the water fronts of English-speaking countries, after which he accompanied them. There was nothing else for him to do, when it came right down to it.

Monk and Ham became involved in a deep, whispered discussion about whether to forgive their pets, who now appeared to want to adopt their respective masters again.

It ended with painful abruptness when the bronze man's aids became aware of gun muzzles protruding from the jungle on either side of the trail.

Lupp's voice said calmly, "I hope you gentlemen don't think for a moment that I won't shoot!"

Chapter XX

PAYMENT IN DEATH

DOC SAVAGE'S five men had no doubts about what Lupp might do. They had been trapped, and they were the more stupefied because Two-bit, the Oriental, had warned them about it.

Two-bit, it now seemed, had been on the level.

Doc's men lifted their hands, and when they saw the number of foes who came out of the jungle with ready guns, were glad they had not tried to fight. All Lupp's gang seemed to be present. More than a dozen.

Two-bit gave Lupp a big, happy smile, said, "This lowly and foolish one got lost. These bad fella glab him, which is what he had coming fol being such clumsy ox."

Lupp gave the Oriental a dark-eyed scowl, opened his mouth, closed it, and said nothing.

Monk and his companions said nothing, either. They almost held their breaths. Two-bit, they were convinced, was all right. And if he put this over, he might help them.

Two-bit apparently put it over.

"Stand still!" Lupp ordered his prisoners.

They were relieved of their weapons, their pockets were emptied, and Lupp's men produced strong cords and applied them to their wrists. Judging from the workmanlike knotting, there were ex-sailors in the gang.

"Shoot that hog and that other thing!" Lupp snarled.

At this, Habeas and Chemistry vanished into the jungle. Two bullets could hardly have gone more swiftly.

Lupp, enraged, turned on the prisoners. "Where is Doc Savage, Kit Merrimore and the Spaces?"

This was the first the prisoners had heard about Doc Savage having encountered the young woman or any one named Space, and their startled expressions undoubtedly did more than their vocal denials to convince Lupp they really did not know where Doc was.

"Well, we're going to keep you alive for a while," Lupp advised them. "You may come in handy."

He barked commands, and the march got started

toward the end of the valley where Ost lay. Lupp had no hesitancy about following the trail. He simply made his captives walk ahead, so that they would fall into any trap of poisoned thorns or hidden arrow-guns which might be planted.

Monk, to keep his mind off possible traps in the trail, asked questions.

"How did you birds get the dirigible off the *Benny Boston?*" the homely chemist wanted to know.

"Velly easy," Two-bit volunteered. "We lun ship aglound on island, lock clew in hold and put boxes on beach. We fix up ailship and——"

"Shut up, you laundryman!" Lupp snarled.

Eventually Monk and the others caught sight of the black overhanging cliff under which Ost was situated. About the same time, they began to hear sounds of shouting and screaming, and to observe a sheet of smoke creeping out from under the face of the cliff.

"I'll bet Savage is having some trouble!" Lupp chuckled gleefully, and made every one put on speed.

HAM, Monk and the other three, anxious and consumed with curiosity to know what was happening, dashed ahead so briskly that it was only by running at full speed and clubbing with gun stocks that Lupp and his men slowed them down. Even after that, they made a brisk pace, and came in sight of the strange city of Ost.

The party ran with their mouths open in astonishment and wonder for a time, and it was only when Lupp managed to stop them that they realized what was happening.

Lupp used field glasses on the smoke pouring out from under the cliff.

"Hah!" he yelled. "They're smoking Savage, that girl, the Spaces and old Goa out of the temple!"

This seemed to be what was happening. An enormous amount of smoke, and probably a great deal of heat, was pouring up from a fire kindled under the temple. The fire had evidently been burning some time, judging from the gigantic column of smoke hanging above the cliff.

Lupp said, "That'll get Savage out of there, if he's in the place. But we can work it as well as them blue mugs, and now is a swell chance to make a surprise attack and clean out the place."

Monk and the others were now lashed to trees, one man to each tree, and a thorough job was done with the tyings, as had been done with their wrist bindings. They could scarcely move when Lupp's men were done, and Lupp assigned a rifleman, a thin fellow with one bad eye and that entirely evil to watch them, making it highly unlikely they would get free.

Lupp and the others rushed off in a charge. Monk promptly emitted a yell for whatever good it would do. It got him knocked senseless, the rifleman seeming to take a pleasure in the job. And the Ostians did not hear it, being too busy jumping and yelling around their fire.

Renny could see, from where he was tied, almost all that happened. And the awful cries told him the rest.

Lupp and his men got through the hole in to the city before they were discovered. Each of them carried a submachine gun or automatic rifle, and apparently, plenty of ammunition. they turned loose.

A roaring as of rain on a great roof came out from under the cliff. The acoustics of the place made the machine-gun roaring hollow sounding.

It was impossible to see over the wall, but the cries told enough. The helpless Ostians must have died by the dozens.

Then the unexpected happened. Lupp and his men appeared, running wildly in flight. Three of them were being carried by the others. These three seemed to have something wrong with their legs.

The Ostians then appeared. But they were not chasing Lupp and his gang. The Ostians seemed to want only to get away from the horrible place.

Something other than the Ostians, then, had routed Lupp. Monk, who had regained his senses, and the others learned what it was when Lupp arrived.

Lupp swore until his face was almost as blue as that of an Ostian.

"Space's rifles were in the temple!" Lupp snarled.

"He and Savage are using them. They didn't use 'em on the Ostians. I guess they weren't in any danger from that fire and smoke. But they sure used them on us!"

"Velly tough," Two-bit said. "Mebbeso cannot get close to cliff evel."

Two-bit did not sound as if he thought it was very tough.

FOUR or five hours now dragged past. None of the Ostians put in an appearance. Things appeared to have become too much for them, and they had hidden out, and were no longer a force to contend with.

Doc Savage showed himself in an aperture which opened in one of the sides of the temple. There seemed to be a number of such openings, fitted with doors so skillfully made that their exact location could not be detected when they were closed.

Doc dropped a line down, a line with a knot every foot or so. Whether or not he intended to descend, no one ever knew. He might have been merely seeing what would happen.

At any rate, Lupp's men cut the rope with bullets before it had stopped swinging.

"We got him penned in there," Lupp said. "But with them rifles, he can keep us away. I happen to know Space had plenty of ammunition when he came to this place."

That seemed to be the impasse.

Renny, Monk and the other three waited with their breaths almost bated for what Lupp was pretty sure to decide to do. He had not mentioned the idea eventually, but it was logical that he would.

He would threaten to shoot them if Doc Savage did not surrender the temple fortress—that strange, suspended building which hung under the cliff for no good reason but that it was made of blocks of lodestone filled with a magnetism that held them to the cliff, which was also of lodestone.

But Lupp was slow getting the idea they feared he would get. Lupp even disappeared later in the day, with two of his men, and was gone for considerable interval. Almost three hours.

Doc Savage's men next observed Lupp close to the walls of Ost, yelling at Doc Savage. The bronze man appeared and yelled back. This shouted exchange continued for several minutes.

The prisoners were too far distant to hear exactly what was said.

Lupp left the vicinity of the Ostian wall, and next appeared before the prisoners wearing a big grin, and followed by two men carrying large boxes which were obviously so heavy that their weight was all the men could stagger under.

Lupp leered, expanded his chest.

"Well," he said, "We made a deal."

THE idea of Lupp making a deal with Doc Savage smacked of the impossible. Monk and the others stuck their ears out and listened.

"You seen me havin' a talk with Savage?" Lupp said.

"Uh-huh," Monk admitted.

"O.K.," Lupp continued. "We made a deal. It's this: I give Savage a share of the treasure and turn you mugs loose, and Savage gets out of Ost, and stays in the jungle until we get clear of this place in the airship."

"Oh!" Monk exploded. "You already got the loot, eh?"

"Of course," Lupp said, looking surprised. "We got that the first thing."

He paused and pointed at the boxes. "There's the share we're gonna give Savage. We're gonna turn you loose, see, and you take it into Savage in the city. Have him examine it if he thinks we're trying to run a whizzer on him."

"Something about this smells," Monk said.

Lupp swore. "You're damned right it smells! But what am I gonna do? I can't have Savage gettin' out——"

He stopped, looked confused.

"So there is a catch!" Monk growled.

Lupp glared at him. "All right, there is. I don't think Savage and the rest of you will ever be able to make it out of this place. Maybe you will. But if you do, it'll be months from now, and I'll have the swag disposed of and be out of the picture."

That, Monk reflected, sounded more reasonable. The homely chemist swung his arms briskly when he was untied, and was contemplating taking a swing at Lupp for luck when one of the boxes was shoved into his arms. It was a stout pine box, one which had evidently been brought to the valley aboard the dirigible. It was extremely heavy.

The others were untied. Ham, Johnny and Long Tom were handed boxes. This was all of the boxes.

"I'll help with one of them," Renny rumbled.

"Wait a minute," Lupp said. "I've got something for you to carry."

With that, he walked over to Two-bit, the wily Oriental, and with a sudden blow of his revolver barrel, knocked Two-bit senseless.

"He thinks he's been kidding me," Lupp said sourly. "But I've had a hunch he was working for Space all the time."

Renny picked up Two-bit. Monk, Ham, Long Tom and Johnny carried their boxes.

They were permitted to walk to the strange, black metropolis of Ost.

Monk called a parting word over his shoulder. "You'll probably try to shoot us down when we leave!"

"You can trust me," Lupp said smugly.

WHEN Monk and the others had staggered out of earshot with their burdens, one of Lupp's men addressed his chief.

"They're suspicious as hell," he said.

Lupp chuckled. "Sure. But not suspicious of the right thing."

"But Savage may guess the truth!"

"Unlikely. I told Savage the boxes would contain food, arms and ammunition, and a part of the treasure which we had already recovered. I told him he could take them and leave the valley, or fight it out, as he pleased, providing he would leave the city. He agreed to leave the city to get his men released."

"Oh," said the other. "Then he won't suspect. But I thought the treasure was all in that hanging temple?"

"The bulk of it is," Lupp agreed. "But there is a little scattered around over the valley in little shrines. Savage and even old Goa will think we have gathered that."

The other man shivered. "But maybe Goa is mind reader enough to detect the trick?"

Lupp shook his head, cursed softly. "Goa can read minds, but he has to be face to face with the subject, then I think he judges quite a bit by facial expressions. But don't think for a minute that he can't project or teleport his thoughts, crazy as that sounds. He made them sailors on the *Benny Boston* think they saw this whole——"

He stopped to watch Monk and the others file through the narrow aperture in the wall of Ost. A few moments later, Doc Savage swung down from the hanging temple. Goa followed the bronze man more slowly. Then Martin Space, his wife, and lastly, Kit Merrimore.

"Swell!" Lupp growled. "A perfect set-up! Now, all we've got to do is wait until they open the boxes!"

"You sure there'll be no slip?"

"No chance. There's TNT enough in them boxes to sink half a dozen battleships. And the moment one of those boxes is opened, an electric contact will be closed and set it off."

The other nodded, moistened his lips. "How did you get wise to the chink?"

"Oh, he's probably all right."

"What?"

"Sure. I just figured I'd get rid of him. Never did like the whelp. Too chicken-hearted. During that business with the machine guns a while ago, he claimed his gun jammed. I think he jammed it himself. Afraid to kill anybody."

They stood there conversing, mainly about what their swag would bring. Lupp, on his previous sojourn into the valley, seemed to have appraised the treasure rather closely, and he had definite ideas about what the venture should pay.

"Beauty of it is we won't have to deal through fences," he explained. "Nobody'll know how we got it.

I should say five or six million, anyway, and maybe more."

Mention of so much money made the listener a little flushed.

But the roaring explosion which came an instant later made him pale again.

Chapter XXI

THE TRAP

LUPP was running an instant after he heard the blast. He kept in the open, and could see all that happened.

The boxes, he decided, had been taken into one of the pyramid black houses at the end of the city wall for opening. The house came apart, and the pieces jumped high, buffeted about and licked and split by tongues of flame.

Dust and smoke came up to engulf the stones while they tumbled about in the air, and the whole cliff trembled, and a few big fragments came loose and ran bouncing down.

The roar, strangely enough, was not a single sound, but a booming series of them, due to some strange, echoing effect of the cavity under the cliff.

Lupp wrenched to a stop, and waited until a few rocks had come rolling toward him and stopped, and the dust had lifted to show a tumbled mass of black stone where the house and that portion of the wall had been.

"Come on!" Lupp yelled at his men.

They scrambled wildly over the mass of blasted rock, some portions of which were still settling, making groaning noises.

Lupp listened to these unpleasant sounds and chuckled.

"I'll bet Savage or some of his crowd are making a few of those!" he declared.

The men got over the mass of stone which had been the house before the explosion.

Lupp saw that the rope was still hanging down from the temple which clung so queerly to the underside of the cavernlike cliff overhang.

"Climb up!" he ordered. "Lower the stuff down. Them fool Ostians may get their nerve back. If we're away before they do, so much the better."

Lupp held the rope, and two of his men climbed. Then greed to see the wealth he knew was above got the best of Lupp, and he yelled at another man to steady the line, and himself started up. The knots were large enough so that it was not at all difficult to climb.

Lupp got ten feet or so up.

A man below yelled, "Hey! Look!"

Lupp looked. And he promptly fell the ten feet back to earth, bruising himself, but hardly noticing. He sprang erect with his gun in his hand.

"Tricked us!" he squawled.

He was apparently right. Doc Savage and all his party had appeared—outside the walls of Ost. Obviously, they had crept out through the narrow city gate while Lupp and his men were clambering joyfully over the blasted remnants of the house.

Doc and his party was furthermore now stationed so as to cover the hole blasted in the wall, as well as the narrow city gate. And they had Martin Space's rifles.

Two of Lupp's men, overly reckless, raced for the hole made by the explosive.

Doc Savage and big-fisted Renny aimed deliberately. Their rifles made noise. They must have made a slight mistake and both aimed at the same target, for one of the two men fell, shot through both legs. The other whirled and fled.

"Get down!" Lupp snarled. "They found out about the explosive and managed to explode the boxes so we would think——"

He stopped, fell to eyeing the blasted remains of the house narrowly. Something struck him. The explosion had seemed amply large when it had occurred, but now that he thought about it, and the power of TNT, he came to a decision.

"They only exploded one box!" he snorted.

Lupp got himself under cover, looked around, and hit on a campaign.

"We'll blow six or seven holes in those houses and the wall!" he yelled. "From them, we can do plenty of good sniping!"

Lupp himself carried hand grenades, and several of his men were likewise equipped. They produced the violent little metal eggs.

"Listen!" a man muttered. "That guy is yellin' at us."

THE fellow meant Doc Savage. The bronze man's powerful voice was plainly audible. He was conveying a warning.

"Do not use your grenades," Doc called, which proved he had heard Lupp's yell. "It is dangerous——"

Lupp gritted, "Who the hell does he think he is!" and began hurling grenades.

They were powerful grenades. The first one rolled into a pyramid house, went off, and lifted the roof and kicked the walls outward. The second upset a line of black wall.

Lupp, looking pleased and enthusiastic, snarled, "These eggs can do plenty!" and let fly a third.

He was right. The grenade could do plenty, and it proceeded to do it—much more than Lupp or any of his men expected. It did what Doc Savage had tried to warn them that it would do.

The bronze man had always adhered to his policy of never taking a human life if it could be avoided, and it was for that reason that he had yelled.

Lupp's grenade lit in a house with the other three boxes of TNT. Doc and his men had set off only one with a small grenade of their own which had contained a time fuse. Doc chanced to have one of these left on his person.

The shock was terrific. It was more of a shock than an explosion, even out where the bronze man and his companions stood. It hurt their ears, even their eyes, with its sudden pressure.

The earth jumped and shook, so that they instinctively doubled over and put their hands on the ground to keep from falling.

A few rock fragments reached as far as the spot where Doc and his aids stood, mostly coming bounding along the ground, and driving them behind trees for safety.

There was a great roaring and grinding after the first smash of the blast, a kind of delayed shock with it, too, as if the explosion had caused something to happen.

"The cliff fell down!" Monk yelled.

MONK was wrong. It was only the temple. But it might as well have been the cliff, for all it meant to Lupp and his men, because they happened to be under the temple at the time it came down.

The sudden shock had been too much for the strange temple sticking, by the force of magnetic attraction, to the underside of the cliff.

"Magnetism," Long Tom, the electrical wizard explained, "can be disturbed by a shock, as any one can prove by taking an ordinary horseshoe magnet and hitting it a sharp blow with a hammer. Sometimes the magnetism will be almost completely destroyed. The shock disturbs the atomic arrangement which causes the magnetic lines of force, and——"

"I should say the fellow most disturbed was Lupp," said Monk, who was a bit callous, and who had been looking around. "Ham found something he claims is all that is left of Lupp, but it looks to me like nothing but a big, greasy mass."

Then Renny came up to explain that only two of Lupp's men were alive.

"They cleared out during the excitement," Renny rumbled.

Monk shouted, "They may try to get the airship——" Remembering he had removed certain essential parts of the airship, the homely chemist looked more relieved.

Renny said, "What you had better worry about is finding those jets for the dirigible Diesels which Lupp's men removed."

Their searching located some of the jets, but others they did not find.

It took the group almost three weeks of rather painstaking work to fashion new Diesel jets out of the materials at hand.

In that interval, the Ostians came around to a more level-headed way of thinking. They accepted the presence of Doc and his men, and agreed to let them depart.

The falling of the temple, the Ostians announced elaborately, must mean that the spiritual power of their deities—another way of describing the magnetism in the lodestone mountain—had relaxed and let the temple fall. Therefore, things should be changed.

The wealth brought with them from their ancient home centuries ago was accursed, and should be handed over to the white men. It was so that it could be handed over to the white men that the deities had relaxed the hold on the temple and let it fall.

Just how much old Goa had to do with this impression getting around among his people was problematical. When Doc went to question Goa, the old fellow had vanished somewhere into the jungle.

Doc Savage spent a good deal of time hunting Goa, desiring greatly to hold lengthy conversation with him, for Goa was the one being the bronze man had ever encountered who had actually accomplished many of the things that the more liberal psychologists and experts on the human brain have admitted possible.

But there was no trace of Goa. He was a sly old fox.

DOC SAVAGE'S men took no part in the Goa hunt. They were occupied with the Diesel jets, and with the jewels and yellow metal which they were collecting from the wreckage of the temple, with the aid of the Ostians.

There was a great deal of the wealth. Even more than they suspected. The value unlucky Lupp had put upon it would not cover more than a fraction of it, because Lupp had never seen the full extent of the trove.

The bronze man's aids had to discard every nonessential part of the dirigible in order to carry the full load.

Doc, having failed to find Goa, did some research on the subject of why all Ostians had blue skins. The solution turned out to be a simple one: A sacred color, blue. So the Ostian simply took all their baths in water which had been dyed with the juice of a berry.

None of the Ostians would consider leaving the valley. They said so in no uncertain language. Furthermore, they insisted that if they never saw any more white men, it would be perfectly all right with them.

"Heck with them," Monk grinned. "Who would want to stay here, anyhow?"

Ham said, "I know what your objection to 'em is, you missing link!"

"What, you shyster?"

"These short-legged, long-armed Ostian girls don't appeal to you."

Monk grinned.

"They were kinda spidery at that," he said.

The dirigible got all of them out of the valley, and most of the way back to civilization. They only had to walk through the jungles for about three weeks after the lifting gas gave out.

DOC SAVAGE

To the world at large, Doc Savage is a strange, mysterious figure of glistening bronze skin and golden eyes. To his fans he is the greatest adventure hero of all time, whose fantastic exploits are unequaled for hair-raising thrills, breathtaking escapes, blood-curdling excitement!

☐	THE EVIL GNOME	2134	$1.25
☐	THE MOUNTAIN MONSTER	2239	$1.25
☐	THE MAN OF BRONZE	6352	$1.25
☐	THE STONE MAN	6419	$1.25
☐	THE BOSS OF TERROR	6424	$1.25
☐	THE THOUSAND HEADED MAN	6471	$1.25
☐	THE RED TERRORS	6486	$1.25
☐	DOC SAVAGE: HIS APOCALYPTIC LIFE	8834	$1.25
☐	THE KING MAKER	10042	$1.25
☐	THE PHANTOM CITY	10119	$1.25
☐	THE MYSTIC MULLAH	10120	$1.25
☐	FEAR CAY	10121	$1.25
☐	LAND OF ALWAYS NIGHT	10122	$1.25
☐	FANTASTIC ISLAND	10125	$1.25
☐	QUEST OF QUI	10126	$1.25

Buy them at your local bookstore or use this handy coupon for ordering: